HER ALIEN WARRIOR PRINCE

WARRIORS OF VALKRED: BOOK 1

Roxie Ray
© 2019
Disclaimer

Contents

Chapter One

Akzun

Why the hell did we have to meet here? Why tonight?

I peered out the nearest window as I asked myself this question for perhaps the hundredth time, trying to focus on the vastness of space outside the station – distant stars twinkling in an endless black sea.

My people, the Valkred, are naturally drawn to darkness. We seek it out, thrive on it, revel in it. To us, shadows are extensions of ourselves. They are our shields and our weapons, as surely as the blade-resistant body armor we wear and the blasters hanging from our belts. They comfort us, nourish us, almost as much as the blood we consume to survive.

And what is space, after all, but an infinity of shadows? A place where even the blaze of the most brilliant sun is swiftly snuffed out by the darkness that presses in from every side, and stretches to eternity?

It's no wonder the Valkred dominated this sector for so many centuries...until the Mana rose up to challenge us for supremacy.

I sighed heavily, thinking of the countless casualties lost in battles with the Mana over the last three decades. No clan on the Valkred home world had been spared from the slaughter. All the members of our race had grieved for fathers, sons, brothers, friends, and mates. I had personally attended the memorial services of five cousins, two uncles, a nephew, and dozens of companions from my youth.

I remembered each one, bitterly and far too vividly. And after every one, I offered up a silent prayer to the stars that it would be the last.

Now, finally, it seemed as though my prayers might have been answered. M'ruvev, the new leader of the Mana, had sent a transmission saying he was willing to negotiate a peace treaty. He set the time and place for our meeting – and despite my misgivings about both, I agreed to his terms in the name of diplomacy and the prevention of additional loss of Valkred life.

But why here, damn it? And why tonight?

"Come now, Akzun," Zark chuckled, slapping me on the shoulder good-naturedly. "You know perfectly well why M'ruvev insisted on meeting you here, and why he chose this night in particular. So stop repeating the same thoughts over and over, before you give me a headache!"

I let out a humorless laugh. My race's telepathic abilities were a blessing at some times, and a curse at others. "Still poking around in my mind without my permission, Zark? I thought that would stop when I was ordained Blood Ruler of Valkred."

Zark raised an eyebrow sardonically, running his pale fingers through his curly purple hair. His dark green eyes twinkled with mirth. "Then you're a bigger fool than I ever gave you credit for. It's a brother's prerogative to go rummaging through his sibling's things at will."

Torqa, my advisor, stared Zark down stonily, her arms folded across her chest. "The Blood Ruler's private thoughts are to be shared at his discretion, not stolen and snickered at by his underlings. Such transgressions are considered acts of treason. If you think Akzun is incapable of punishing those close to him for that sort of thing, ask Elrisa."

I held up a hand to silence her, suppressing a shudder at the mention of Elrisa's name. That wound was still a bit too fresh for me to contemplate. "There's no need to bring that up, Torqa. Zark is accustomed to taking certain liberties where I'm concerned."

Torqa nodded, but she was clearly displeased at being reprimanded. "I apologize, Ruler. I only seek to protect you in all things, as ever."

"I know. And your loyalty is appreciated...if somewhat vociferous. Not that I can blame you. I suppose we're all a bit on edge today."

I turned back to the window, but privately reached out to Zark telepathically, connecting our minds so we could communicate without being overheard. *All right, so let's hear it. Why do you believe M'ruvev chose the Cexiea Station for our peace summit? A member of our race runs it, so it can hardly be considered neutral ground. And it's full of thieves, killers, smugglers, raiders, and every other sort of outlaw in the cosmos...not ideal in terms of ensuring security for all concerned.*

I could see Zark's reflection in the thick, blast-proof glass, his lupine features so similar to my own. He grinned, running his tongue over his fangs – an old familiar gesture, one he'd perfected when we were children and our permanent canine teeth started to come in. A way for him to remind me that his were slightly longer. He'd always had a competitive nature.

First of all, M'ruvev didn't just choose Cexiea, Zark thought at me with a smirk. *He specifically chose this nightclub – The Vein. And the fact that you chose telepathy rather than words to discuss this with me proves that you know exactly what his reasons were. He wants you distracted, off-guard, so he'll have the tactical advantage during the negotiations. He must have his suspicions regarding the onset of your...condition.*

Impossible! I tried to keep my expression neutral so Torqa wouldn't suspect that I was conversing with Zark, but inwardly, I felt as though my worst fears were being confirmed. *You're the only one I've told about the bloodlust. How could he possibly know?*

The Mana have spies everywhere. You know that better than most. Unlike Torqa, Zark knew better than to reference Elrisa directly – he knew the pain that memory caused me. Still he wouldn't let me forget it. *And even though you're doing your best to hide the symptoms, brother, someone with a well-trained eye might still be able to guess what you're going through. You've been twitchy, distant, ill-tempered. Your pallor has started to shift from white to an ashy gray, and your gums are receding. Your hair is losing its luster. All of this is still in the early stages, and could conceivably be blamed on stress or fatigue. So far, that's what's kept anyone on our home world from challenging your rule. But if the wrong person knew what to look for...*

I suppose I didn't realize how bad it had gotten, I admitted. *So you think M'ruvev specifically chose The Vein so I'd be surrounded with blood slaves...and chose a non-auction night so I'd be unable to slake my thirst by purchasing one of them?*

Zark tilted his head slightly to indicate our surroundings. *I've certainly heard worse plans. You have to admit, this place is full of distractions*.

I looked around, conceding his point. The club was dim, low-ceilinged, and the light fixtures were all filtered crimson – a subtle touch that made every Valkred who entered feel like they were in the final stages of bloodlust, swimming through a red ocean of throbbing bodies waiting to be drained.

Most of the patrons were Valkred, like myself, but there were others as well: a crew of reptilian Krote scavengers sat drinking in a corner, loudly singing a space shanty and banging their mugs of Vraklian Nova Ale on the table with each new chorus. A pair of white-furred Drekkir who were placing bets on a game of Six-Teeth, scattering a half-dozen ivory molars on the surface of the bar and chittering excitedly at the carved symbols that came up. There was even a lone Lunian male staring at the entrance, the ghostly glow of his skin cutting through the sweaty, smoky, murky air of the place like a beacon – a rare sight on a station full of brigands and cutthroats, to be sure.

And there were the Earthlings.

They, of course, were not in The Vein to drink and socialize. Rather, they were captured and brought here as laborers and living decorations – serving drinks, cleaning up messes, and titillating the clientele with their attractive appearances. The ones with black collars were available for purchase as sexual partners, and wore scandalously revealing outfits. The ones with red collars wore clothing, which revealed more specific areas of their anatomies: major arteries to indicate that they could be bought as blood slaves.

The sight of them immediately made my mouth dry. So tempting, and so out of reach. I had never felt so thirsty in my life. The bloodlust was a syndrome that only took hold of members of the Valkred species as they began to reach middle age, and at just under a hundred years old, it was natural for it to begin to affect me.

Natural, but damned inconvenient.

I can't believe M'ruvev would attempt to gain an unfair advantage over me by resorting to such base trickery, I thought to Zark. *Despite the hostilities between our peoples, I had always considered him a friend*.

I'm sure if Torqa could hear us, Akzun, she'd remind you of her favorite saying: "If you have a friend who is a Mana…"

"…Then you don't have a friend," I finished with him tiredly. *Not exactly the most auspicious beginning to a peace conference, is it, brother?*

No, I think not. And speaking of the Mana… He nodded to the window, and I followed his gaze.

The Mana flagship Aquavor approached the station: huge and slug-like, essentially a miniature ocean contained by an impenetrable membrane of armored fibers, glowing blue and pulsating gently as it moved serenely through space. It was surrounded by half a dozen tiny escort ships, insectile and iridescent as they buzzed in tight formation around their charge. The sight reminded me of the Gorvyan Slime-Leeches of my home planet, drifting through the swamps with clouds of smaller blood parasites in their wake, waiting to feed on whatever dregs the fat worms left behind.

I felt both Zark and Torqa bristle as M'ruvev and his contingent entered The Vein. I tried to appear stoic, but the wings beneath my clothes fluttered apprehensively against my back, their feathers standing on end. I forced my mouth into a smile, stepping forward and bowing slightly. "M'ruvev. It's been a long time."

M'ruvev's scaly lips pulled back into a grin, his fish-like eyes peering up at me. His bluish skin – and that of his companions – was still damp and clammy from swimming around in their ship.

"It's good to see you again, Akzun," he replied, his voice gurgling gently from the water-breathing apparatus hooked up to his flapping gills. "Hopefully, if these peace talks succeed, we'll be able to visit each other far more frequently."

"If you're really interested in the success of this summit, you might have chosen someplace quieter for us to meet. The Vein isn't exactly the most conducive environment for discussions such as these."

M'ruvev sized me up, and for a horrible moment, I was certain that Zark was right – that he had found out about my bloodlust somehow, and planned to mention it in front of Torqa (and anyone else who might be listening… after all, Cexiea was full of spies from every civilized race in the galaxy, as well as some who weren't very civilized at all).

Instead, M'ruvev put his webbed hand on my shoulder. "Akzun, despite the war between our races, I've admired you a great deal and considered you a friend," he burbled. "You saved my ship from a pack of Krote corsairs years ago when you could just as easily have left us to fend for ourselves… as such, I'm indebted to you for life, and it is for this reason that I felt I owed you a chance to bargain for peace. But that doesn't mean I had to make it easy for you. After all, how could my people respect me if I didn't use every strategic advantage at my disposal?"

"A fair point," I conceded, gesturing for him to take a seat. "Just as I wouldn't be much of a Blood Ruler if I allowed such tactics to affect me. Shall we begin, then?"

M'ruvev nodded his bald head serenely, sitting down. As I took the seat across from him, Nos, the owner of The Vein, hobbled over to our table with a tray. He was a Valkred as well – but while most of my race is tall, lithe, and graceful, he'd been born with a rare disfiguring condition called Mak'Shrek Syndrome. As a result, his back was hunched, his fingers were long spidery claws, his head was hairless and lumpy, and he had a mouthful of cruel crooked fangs. When he spoke, it was in a sibilant hiss.

"Ah, such a noble group of worthies blesses my humble tavern with their presence!" he drawled, placing drinks in front of each of us. "Welcome, welcome! Lord M'ruvev, please accept this Eukaryotic Ale on the house… it's been aged in a cask for over two and a half centuries, very strong, yes, very pungent. And for Blood Ruler Akzun, a glass of D'Naarican Blood Cider! The plasma in it was distilled from the Ever-Wise Oracle of Travanya. They say that a sip will briefly infuse you with her visions, yes? Quite potent, oh yes, quite rare indeed! Shall we drink a toast to peace in our time, gentlemen?"

M'ruvev and I raised our glasses, clinked them, and drank deeply, our eyes locked. When our glasses were drained, Nos snatched them away greedily, as though he intended to sell them as mementos from the peace talks – which, knowing his level of entrepreneurship, might indeed have been his intention.

As he scuttled into the back room, he shoved a human female server – one with a red collar – toward our table. She picked up a pitcher of water and two glasses and carried them to our table.

I watched her as she approached, my breath lodged in the back of my throat like a Gangryllian Needle-Bat caught in a tree snare.

I couldn't take my eyes off her.

She was short, even for an Earthling, with wide hips and a beautifully full bosom. Her hair was long and reddish-blonde, her eyes were a penetrating shade of brown, and a series of small speckles decorated her delicate, upturned nose – a rare trait for her species, from what I'd been told.

As she quietly placed the pitcher and glasses on the table, I couldn't help but stare at the exposed areas of her skin. I could practically hear the blood rushing through her brachial and femoral arteries, and the faint pulse of her jugular made beads of sweat form on my skin. Her scent filled my nostrils, a heady, musky aroma that sent a sharp tingle down through the core of my body.

It was all I could do to keep from reaching out and grabbing her right there – to take her, drain her, make her mine. My throat felt like sand, and I was seized with a desperate urge to lick my lips...but that would be a sign of weakness before M'ruvev, one I couldn't afford.

She turned and walked back to the bar, her eyes barely meeting mine. I wasn't surprised. Nos trained his slaves to be stared at by the patrons, not to stare back.

"Akzun?" M'ruvev said teasingly, as if on cue. "Are you still with us?"

Look at him, Zark thought at me. *He knows, the smug bastard.*

No, I shot back. *He might suspect, but I refuse to give him the satisfaction of confirming it. Not when we have the upper hand. Not when we're so close to ending this war.*

"Of course," I answered out loud. "Let's proceed, shall we?"

M'ruvev nodded placidly again.

"Now then," I began briskly, trying to banish all thoughts of the woman and regain my focus. "I suppose I should start by pointing out that our ships outnumber yours five to one, and our forces have numerous advantages over yours in terms of where they're stationed. The systems we've seized have given us a significant tactical edge – their locations are more defensible, especially since they allow us to track your armadas before they can get close enough to strike. As such, it seems we Valkred are in a far better position to dictate the terms of this treaty, wouldn't you say?"

"Are you really?" M'ruvev's eyes narrowed, focusing on the pitcher of water between us. As I watched, the fluid inside began to surge and roil, rising in a shimmering column. Then it arched, pulling itself out of the pitcher completely and approaching me slowly. It sprouted a pair of legs, marched toward me like a soldier on a parade ground...then suddenly collapsed into a puddle on the table, splashing the front of my tunic.

I knew about the Mana's elemental ability to control water with their minds – everyone did – but I'd rarely seen it demonstrated before. It was strangely hypnotic, but also unsettling.

"An amusing parlor trick, my aquatic friend," I said. "But I fail to see your point."

He laughed. "My point? I thought it was fairly obvious. A full two-thirds of those valuable captured outposts you were boasting about a moment ago are planets or moons with significant bodies of water. We should know – they once belonged to us. If a significant number of my race were transported to one of these locations… if we were all to use our abilities at once… we could turn entire oceans into weapons and wipe out your armies."

I shook my head, stealing another glance at the Earthling female and hoping it would go unnoticed. Inwardly, I kicked myself for being so distracted. This peace summit had the potential to be one of the most important historical events in Valkred history, and I was jeopardizing it by allowing my bloodlust to control me.

If only I had chosen a mate by now. Or at least a blood slave, to quell the immediacy of these cravings. But I'd been too busy trying to win the war. No, that wasn't true – I had been too arrogant, too certain that I could keep myself under control until the conflict was over. Too afraid of showing weakness in front of the warriors under my command, too apprehensive that one or more of them would take the opportunity to challenge me for the title of Blood Ruler.

Too late now. I'd have to ride it out, no matter what.

But that woman.

She was like the moon, changing the very tides of the blood in my veins with her gravitational pull. Why her? What was so special about her?

It didn't matter. I had to have her. I felt like I couldn't wait another moment.

"An empty threat if ever I've heard one," I pointed out, trying to keep my voice steady. "If you could do such a thing, you would have by now. And as I said, our sentry forces would spot you long before you reached us."

"You assume that our status in this regard has remained unchanged," M'ruvev answered. "That, for example, we have not perfected cloaking technology for our vessels which would allow us to bypass your sentries. Or that our spies have not located and secured one or more individuals with the power of psymora."

Psymora. Just hearing the word sent a chill up my spine, as it did to many throughout the galaxy. It was common knowledge that there were certain people of various races who could manipulate time itself – freeze it in its tracks, or skip forward and backward across it like a stone across a lake's surface. Such power was frightening to contemplate, and too dangerous for one person to have.

Yet sometimes, they did.

"You're bluffing," I insisted.

"Am I? Very well. If you require proof..." M'ruvev activated his communication device, speaking into it. "M'ruvev to Aquavor. Proceed with the demonstration, please." He turned back to me.

I looked out the window at the Mana flagship – just in time to watch it shimmer briefly, then vanish.

"That's a trick, a hologram. It must be." I touched the button on my own communicator. "Akzun to Angel's Wrath. Confirm the presence of the Aquavor at once."

There was a pause, and then the voice of Commander Koro responded uneasily: "We are unable to confirm, Blood Ruler. There are no engine signatures, no energy traces from weapons or shield systems, no spatial mass displacement. As far as we can tell, sir, they're just...gone."

I turned to M'ruvev. "Where is it?"

M'ruvev shrugged. "Cloaked? Phased? Hidden in the future, the past, an alternate dimension? Cutting through open space toward your precious home world undetected, like a knife slicing toward your throat? The answer, my dear Akzun, is for me to know… and for you to find out the hard way, if you insist on this posturing. What I've just shown you might not necessarily win the war for us immediately, but it can easily be used to escalate the hostilities between the Valkred and the Mana, drawing it out indefinitely. Or you can agree to the terms I've come up with, and we can end this destructive conflict right here and now. The choice is yours."

He produced a tablet with a list of terms, sliding it across the table toward me.

As I reviewed the data, I had to admit that his demands seemed reasonable. The major planets and lunar colonies we'd taken from the Mana would be returned to them, and the smaller outposts and stations would be negotiated on a case-by-case basis. All prisoners of war would be returned to their respective races. Trade would be re-established between the Valkred and Mana, with a steep but temporary tariff imposed on Valkred's imports and exports as a punitive measure for the damages inflicted during the war. And talks would continue, with the goal of forging a lasting military alliance.

Still, I didn't want to capitulate right away. I wanted to offer at least a bit of resistance, try to bargain for a stronger position – strike the tariff from the list, for example, or demand that the Mana restore our own captured territories to us as well.

I wanted to do those things. I wanted to look strong in front of my people, especially since I knew any Valkred or Mana onlookers in the club would quickly share the details of this interaction.

But I couldn't.

I was sweating harder now, and it was taking every ounce of self-control not to tremble openly. My heart felt like it would go supernova in my chest at any moment and obliterate me. The bloodlust was simply too strong. The human girl was too close, her pheromones mocking me, twisting my insides into knots.

I could either agree to M'ruvev's terms and end the summit – and with it, the long-standing feud that had claimed too many lives to count – or I could break down in front of him completely and lose everything: the war, my position as Blood Ruler, and very probably, my life.

"Your terms are acceptable," I replied through gritted teeth. "From this point forward, no Valkred shall fire upon a Mana ship or outpost as long as both sides honor the treaty."

"I'm delighted to hear that." M'ruvev stood, and I followed suit. "You'll see, Akzun. This day will be remembered as a triumph for both of our races. Now that diplomatic relations have been restored, there will be no limit to what we can accomplish together."

"Agreed. Now if you'll excuse me, I have some rather urgent business to discuss with our host." I turned and walked toward Nos, trying to keep my stride casual, even though every cell in my body wanted to break into a run, to throw all of my money at him in exchange for the woman and drag her to my ship at once.

"Yes, I imagine you do," M'ruvev murmured under his breath.

Chapter Two

Carly

I hated the dress.

I realized I must have been in a state of shock so deep I couldn't even fully understand it. Just three days ago, I'd been on Earth, working my new waitressing gig at Gianni's Pizza and Wings in Scottsdale.

On Earth – as though that had been a distinction worth making, before, as though I'd ever even *dreamed* that there were alien races on other planets like in those science fiction flicks my dad used to watch on the classic movie channels when I was a kid.

I never gave any thought as to whether extraterrestrials and their flying saucers might actually exist out there somewhere. Life on my own planet always seemed strange enough to me.

Especially after I lost my job fixing engines and riveting airplane parts for Cumulus Aeronautics.

I'd been there for almost four years. I was one of their best mechanics. *Can't fix it? Give it to Carly.* That was what everyone there used to say. I'm not sure why I was so naturally good at it – ever since I was a little girl, I'd always been obsessed with taking things apart and putting them back together again, figuring out how they worked. With the right background, I could have been an engineer in my own right… but unfortunately, Earth was a place of haves and have-nots, and no matter how hard I worked or what grades I got in school, people never let me forget which one I was. When I was accepted for the mechanic job, I was told in no uncertain terms how lucky I'd been to get it.

Those were the best years of my life. The title and pay were low, but the respect I got from my co-workers and supervisors made it all worthwhile. I loved wearing overalls and having engine grease under my fingernails. I loved the smell of metal and oil, of sweat and fuel and sunshine on a hot tarmac. I loved looking up into the sky, seeing the contrails behind the gleaming aircraft, and knowing I was the reason they were flying.

Sometimes, on my days off (which were rare), I'd sit in the airport and just watch people preparing to board for parts unknown. I'd look at the businessmen, the students, the families, and I'd think: *Once you're aboard and in the air, if you have a moment, look out the window. See those fingerprints on the wing? They're mine. Hear the gentle whine of the engine? I did that for you. Wherever you're going, you'll be getting there safely because of me.*

I knew those kinds of thoughts were silly, not to mention more than a little arrogant. But I didn't care. It made me happy – it gave me a sense of purpose, of importance. It reminded me that it didn't matter where I came from, or how low my status was. I could still make a difference. I could make the world a better place for others. Nothing could take that away from me.

Or so I thought.

Then my shift manager retired, and I was assigned a new one: Lars Morganstern, a man who looked like a warthog and stank like a dumpster on a hundred-degree day. A man who didn't know his ass from his elbow when it came to putting planes together – who only got the job because his uncle was the company's chief financial officer.

A man who couldn't resist staring at my tits and making lewd jokes every time he was around me.

I could see that my co-workers wanted to come to my defense, but they didn't dare, and I didn't blame them. He could have fired any of them with a snap of his fat fingers, and among the lower classes, jobs had never been more scarce.

One evening, Lars dismissed everyone except me – told me there was a new shipment of engine parts he wanted me to take a look at and inventory.

I wasn't stupid. I knew the real reason why he wanted to be alone with me. I saw the whole scene play out in my head beforehand, but that didn't stop any of it from happening: His sausage fingers feeling me up the moment my back was turned. His scowl when I told him to knock it off. The look of surprise and pain on his piggish face when he refused to stop and I kicked him squarely in the groin.

The next day, there was a pink slip waiting for me in my locker. None of the other workers could make eye contact. They were too ashamed that there was nothing they could have done to stop any of it.

I was fortunate to get the server job at Gianni's a few days later; most people from the lower classes who lost their jobs stayed out of work for months. I loathed carrying trays and getting yelled at by rich assholes for not bringing their food quickly enough, but what else could I do? I had to live, after all. And with no other jobs available, I figured I'd better get used to it… even though every time I heard a plane overhead, I wanted to cry.

Then one night, as I was walking back to my shitty studio apartment after my shift, I saw a light in the sky ahead. It was getting closer and closer, but as I squinted up at it, I couldn't place it. Its movements were too smooth and nimble, too precise, to be a plane. A helicopter? Perhaps, but then why couldn't I hear the rotors? The most obvious answer seemed to be a drone, but drones never came to the low-class area where I lived – no one there could afford to order the kinds of goods that delivery drones would bring, and the law enforcement drones had stopped caring about what went on there years ago.

Whatever it is, I'd thought to myself, *I'd sure love to get a closer look at it.*

There was a sudden flash of light, a feeling like the ground was being yanked away from under my feet – and the next thing I knew, I was on this damn space station, being ordered around in broken English by a grotesque ghoul of a bartender who called himself Nos.

Wearing this fucking dress, which I hated.

Yes, I was terrified to be surrounded by bizarre creatures that babbled and gurgled and roared at each other – and at me – in what seemed like a hundred different languages. Yes, I was frightened by the thought of how far I must have been from home, and whether I'd ever see it again. Yes, I was scared to death that I'd get someone's drink order wrong and be eaten alive or vaporized by some laser beam, or whatever the hell these alien bastards did when they got angry. When I let myself think about those things, really internalize them, it felt like my brain was going to crack in half… like I'd start crying and screaming and never stop.

If I did, though, I'd probably be severely punished for it by Nos.

Which is probably why my mind wouldn't let me fully focus on anything except the goddamn ugly, skimpy, annoyingly slutty dress they were forcing me to wear.

The collar was uncomfortable, sure, but the dress made me feel like I was being wholly robbed of my identity. On Earth, I'd never worn dresses. They'd always seemed silly, impractical, even a little demeaning. Even at my waitressing job, I was allowed to wear jeans and a t-shirt.

If I were out of the dress, and feeling like my usual, resourceful self, maybe I could have thought my way out of this situation – found some way to escape. In it, I felt helpless and lost.

As I brought a pitcher of water to a table, I could feel one of the patrons sitting at it staring at me openly. He was tall, thin, and pale, with bluish-silver hair and a vaguely pointed face that reminded me of a timber wolf. Most of the patrons in this bar seemed to be the same species as him; I thought I'd heard them referred to as "Valkyries" or something like that, which didn't seem to make much sense, since the Valkyries were women and many of these aliens looked like they were probably male. (Then again, for all I knew, genders weren't the same out here in space.)

But there was something about the one staring at me… something I couldn't quite put my finger on. An air of nobility in the way he carried himself, as though he were some authority figure. This was confirmed by the deference the other members of his race seemed to show him. Even Nos looked like he was eager to kiss this guy's ass, bringing him drinks personally and fawning over him.

Still, I was determined not to stare at him as I set the pitcher down, no matter how intense his gaze was. After all, for all I knew, staring back at him was considered an insult on his planet.

As I continued to carry drinks to the customers, I stole a few more glances at him. He was flanked by two other members of his species (servants? Advisors? Bodyguards?), and involved in what looked like heavy negotiations with something that seemed to be part man, part fish. Were they bargaining for some item? Exchanging valuable information? Trading insults?

For perhaps the thousandth time since I'd been abducted – "abducted," I couldn't believe I was actually using that word to describe what happened to me, like someone on the cover of a supermarket tabloid – I wished I could at least partially understand some of the languages these creatures spoke.

Suddenly, I felt a small hand grope my ass, right where Lars had once grabbed it. I turned and saw a short, round alien covered in thick white fur. Its fingers were stubby, eyes glowing electric blue, and its mouth was sideways and extended halfway down its chest. When its lips moved, I could see rows of tiny teeth that looked like zippers.

"*Cheeble-deep!*" it squeaked, giving my bottom another squeeze.

I tried to move myself away from him, but he followed, continuing to grab at me.

"*Chee-bee! Bee-hee-beep!*" it chittered insistently.

"No," I said, waving my hands at him (and hoping he'd understand the universal gesture for "get away”).

He shook his head, lunging forward and pawing at my breasts. *“Heep-beeble-dee! Bee-deeblebip!”*

Something inside me snapped. Whoever these people were, whatever their reason had been for kidnapping me from my home planet, whatever stupid outfit they dressed me in – *they couldn't take away who I was,* any more than Lars could by firing me. I wasn't some defenseless bimbo who'd let men feel me up without standing up for myself. I was *Carly Love*, goddamn it, and I'd make anyone who treated me like an object pay dearly for it, no matter *what* the consequences.

I was about to give the fur ball a taste of the same medicine I'd given Lars – my leg was tensed, ready for me to bring my knee up sharply between this alien lecher's legs – when another human woman rushed over. She was tall, with blue eyes, long brown hair, and an athletic build.

“Chibbip,” she said to the alien, putting her hands up in a placating gesture and bowing deeply. *“Chibbip-cha.”*

The furry critter considered her for a moment, then let out a low growl, stalking away.

“What did you say to him?” I asked her.

“The only phrase I know in Drekkir. Roughly translated, it means, 'We're sorry, please don't do us harm.' It comes in handy. I'm Miranda, by the way.”

She extended her hand, and I shook it. “Carly. Nice to meet you, even if it's...well, here. What did he want?”

Miranda raised an eyebrow at me good-naturedly. “Come on, you know damn well what he wanted. Just like it was pretty obvious what you wanted to do about it. It wouldn't have worked, believe me. First of all, kicking the Drekkir between the legs doesn't do any good. Their genitals are located in their gizzards. And second, trying to harm the customers will only get you killed. Nos doesn't tolerate that. He can't risk pissing off any of the patrons. Bad for his business, especially when auction night is only a couple of days from now.”

“Auction night? What the hell is that?”

She sighed, pointing to her black collar. “That's where we get sold to the highest bidder. That's what we're wearing these for… to advertise whether we'll be offered up as sex slaves or blood slaves. Black means sex slave. Lucky me, I guess, huh? Sex slaves can go to anyone, but blood slaves are exclusively bought by Valkreds.” She pointed to the pale man in the corner who'd been staring at me earlier… who was *still* peering at me covertly, even as he spoke with the fish-person. “Those are Valkreds. They're basically space vampires. They need blood to survive, so they buy people like us to use as sustainable food sources. The good news is, whether they buy us for blood or sex, it's in their best interests to keep us alive and healthy for as long as possible.”

My heart stopped. I couldn't believe what I was hearing. “We can't just wait around for that to happen! What the fuck are we going to do? How can we escape?”

She shrugged. “Honey, if I knew how to escape, you'd be talking to an empty collar right now. From what I can tell, there's nothing we can do but wait… and hope that whoever buys us isn't too bad. Everything else is completely beyond our control. I mean, maybe you could try to scope out the clientele in advance, find someone who seems nicer than the others, flirt a little so they'll go out of their way to bid on you. But honestly, that's just about impossible if you don't understand their languages."

Nos appeared next to Miranda, clapping his long-fingered hands together impatiently. "No more talk! You work now! Work harder! Faster!" He gestured to a tray of drinks on the bar.

"Better get to it," Miranda said, picking up the tray. "Try to read their body language. It's not foolproof, but it's better than nothing, right?"

"Thanks for the advice," I replied in a small voice.

I stole another glance at the Valkred who'd been looking at me, just in time to see him stand up and walk over to Nos. His teeth were bared, and I could see his long fangs. The sight made me shiver. I couldn't help but imagine them puncturing my throat. Would it hurt? Or would he put me in some kind of trance first, like Dracula in an old B-movie? Would my blood spurt and gush everywhere, staining his lips, his face? Or would he be able to swallow it all neatly as it pumped out of me, without spilling a drop?

The Valkred began speaking to Nos in their native language in a low, urgent tone. Both of them were looking at me. Were they talking about me? What were they saying?

"You are correct," a deep voice behind me intoned. "They are indeed discussing you."

I turned and saw a tall alien with pale, glowing skin. He was sitting at the bar, his long fingers steepled together.

"You… speak English?" I asked breathlessly.

He nodded slowly. "I speak many languages. It's a hobby of mine. The entire cosmos would function far more smoothly if only we would all take a bit more time and effort to properly understand each other, don't you agree?"

"I guess so," I replied lamely. "So what are they saying about me?"

"Much as I might wish to comfort you with my answer, I fear I can only confirm your worst apprehensions. Akzun – who, it bears mentioning, has the distinction of being Blood Ruler of the Valkred – wishes to purchase you as a blood slave."

I swallowed hard. "I thought the auction wasn't for a couple of days."

"Again, you are correct. However, Akzun appears to be unconcerned with such trivial details, and insists that he must buy you immediately. He is… most vehement in his desire for you. Not that I can blame him. You are most attractive, certainly. For an Earthling, of course."

Nos was shaking his head vigorously, clearly challenging Akzun.

"Now Nos is pointing out that if he were to suddenly start allowing patrons to buy slaves from him on non-auction nights, it would throw his entire business into chaos," the glowing alien said wistfully. "I can sympathize. Running such an establishment cannot be an easy venture. One must establish a clear set of rules in all matters of great importance, and one must adhere to them strictly, or else one invites anarchy, with all of its unruly byproducts, don't you think?"

This time, I didn't bother answering. While I appreciated the translation, this guy's weird philosophical musings were starting to get on my nerves, especially since it looked like my life and future were on the line.

The one called Akzun slammed his fist on the bar, hissing a string of scary-sounding words at Nos.

"Oh my," the alien next to me said, shaking his head sadly. "Akzun says he will not be denied, and has threatened to tear off Nos's fingers and forcibly deposit them in a most uncomfortable orifice if he doesn't agree to sell you. Such violence is wholly gratuitous in a wondrous galaxy that's capacious enough for all races to coexist in harmony, wouldn't you say?"

"Sure, yeah, definitely. But *what's Nos saying?*"

The alien tilted his shimmering head, listening closely. His eyes widened. "By the stars! You will be pleased to know that Nos has placed your monetary value at a quarter of a million rula... a sizable sum indeed! No doubt he believes that Akzun will be put off by the exorbitant amount, and will let the matter rest."

My pulse was thrumming in my temples as I stared at the two Valkred, hoping the alien was right, praying that Akzun would simply walk away. With a couple of days left until the auction, maybe I could still find a way out of all this. Maybe there was some possibility of escape, something that Miranda hadn't thought of...

Akzun reached into a hidden pocket of his outfit and withdrew a thick stack of paper bills, tossing them down on the bar.

My stomach sank through the floor.

"I suppose congratulations are in order," the glowing alien said mildly. "After all, it is not every day that one enters the service of the Blood Ruler of Valkred. To many, it would be considered quite an honor... though I suppose there are few in your position who would see it that way. Still, in a vast and intriguing cosmos filled with such a variety of beings, I suppose many things some see as absolute truths might be viewed by others simply as a matter of perspective, would you concur?"

Akzun was moving toward me swiftly, purposefully, his dark eyes gleaming in the red light of the bar. Behind him, Nos was greedily thumbing through the stack of bills, licking his fangs eagerly.

"Incidentally," the alien added, "if you're inclined to attempt some sort of escape, I suppose this might be the best time to do so. There aren't many places on Cexiea where one such as you would be able to successfully hide, let alone find a way off this station. On the other hand, in a universe of such infinite and exquisite possibilities, anything that can be thought can be accomplished, is that not so?"

I turned and ran toward the exit, my mind racing.

I had no idea what the rest of the station looked like – but based on the generally seedy nature of the bar's clientele, I had to believe there were plenty of dark corners and hidden spaces to take shelter in, if only I could find them in time. Maybe I could scrape and scrounge in the shadows like a rat until I could find a way to stow away on a ship, one that might bring me close to Earth, close enough to find a way home…

As I dashed ten feet outside the bar's entrance, I could see that the corridors of the space station were indeed narrow and dark, with sections of the bulkhead left open to reveal ducts, shafts, tubes, and wires. There *were* plenty of places for me to hide, places to burrow in and bide my time until I could find a path to freedom.

Then Akzun's pale fingers locked onto my upper arm like an iron vise, and he began dragging me in the opposite direction.

"Stop it!" I screamed. "Let me go!"

But he remained silent, staring straight ahead as he pulled me along. And why not? We didn't speak the same language, and even if we had, he'd bought me. As far as he was concerned, I was his property now, and that was the end of it.

I thought about his fangs sinking into my flesh again, and felt like I might faint.

Chapter Three

Akzun

"Let go of me, goddamn it! Stop! I refuse to be manhandled like this, you alien asshole!"

As I dragged the human woman toward the airlock where my ship was docked, she continued to shriek and squeal like a Korbeq Spider-Rat in a trap. I disregarded it – just as I ignored the curious looks from the Valkred and other races on the station, who gaped at us as we passed by. No doubt they were surprised (and envious) that I had been allowed to purchase a blood slave before the date of the auction.

Fine, I thought. *Let them go pay Nos a quarter of a million rula to shop early. A few more customers like me, and the gnarled old bastard of a barkeep can retire early and buy his own private moon.*

The more the woman screamed and resisted, the more tempted I was to speak to her in her own language, to tell her to keep quiet and stop struggling. But why bother? At this stage, I knew it would only be a waste of time. She'd bicker and threaten and cajole, and it would only delay my bringing her to the ship.

Later – when she'd been properly secured in my home – I would reveal that I was able to speak and understand Earth English. Then she'd understand fully that there would be no escape for her, and we could move on to more meaningful topics, like where she'd come from and how long she'd been on Cexiea.

As we approached the airlock, I stopped for just a few precious moments, holding the woman in place firmly as I gazed out the observation window at my ship: The Angel's Wrath.

No matter how many times I saw it, the majesty of it – the knowledge that it was mine to command – still took my breath away.

Large and smooth, ivory-colored and cone-shaped, like a giant tooth extracted from the mouth of some ancient and terrible predator. It had been the proud flagship of almost a dozen Blood Rulers before me, and it was still every bit as fast and formidable as it had been the day of its christening. The outer armor resembled carved enamel, but was in fact ultra-dense reflective marble that had been carefully shaped and chiseled to make lower-spectrum laser blasts bounce off like harmless beams of light.

And the higher-spectrum blasts? Well, that was what the Wrath's overlapping energy shields were for, just as its pulse-mortar tubes and mounted plasma disruptors were for punishing any who dared fire upon such a magnificent vessel.

I heard the woman's breath catch in her throat, and turned to see that she was staring at the ship as well, her eyes wide, her mouth open. Good. At least she had an appropriate eye for beauty.

Commander Koro met me at the airlock, trying to hide his curiosity at my companion. "My apologies, sir. I was unaware that we would be taking on a passenger. Shall I have quarters prepared for her?"

"No." The word was out of my mouth before I could stop myself – but in that moment, it seemed unthinkable to let the woman out of my sight. "She'll be on the command deck, where I can keep an eye on her."

Koro nodded without hesitation. "Very good, sir. Would you like me to fetch a pair of manacles to secure her, so she won't attempt to tamper with any of our systems?"

"That won't be necessary. I'll make sure she doesn't cause any trouble." Again, my own motivations were puzzling to me. Why wouldn't I want her shackled as a safety precaution? Perhaps I felt it would be a sign of weakness, that it would be a greater show of strength in front of my crew for me to keep control of her without them. Perhaps I felt it would put her more at ease, make her easier to deal with later.

Or perhaps there was some other reason – one I didn't want to admit, even to myself. One that was somehow tied to the strange urgency I'd felt about purchasing her before anyone else could.

I could have come back for a blood slave on the night of the actual auction, if I'd wanted. For that matter, now that hostilities with the Mana had ceased, I could have gone to a different auction to purchase one – an auction on the Valkred home world, or one of the other outposts in our empire. What's more, it would have cost a tiny fraction of what I'd paid for this woman.

So why her? Why hadn't I been able to stop myself? Even in the grip of bloodlust, it still seemed like peculiar – and frankly, desperate – behavior. I worried about whether the crew would think less of me for it.

Still, too late to fret about such things now.

"Are Zark and Torqa already aboard?" I asked.

"Yes, sir."

"Then set a course for Valkred Prime at once, maximum speed." I marched the woman past him and through the dark, dimly-lit corridor.

When we reached the low-ceilinged flight deck with its illuminated crimson control panels, I took my seat in the command chair and gestured for her to sit next to me. She hesitated, then slowly sat down, inching as far away from me as possible – as though that would protect her from me, when the time came.

The engines rumbled beneath us, and The Angel's Wrath pulled away from Cexiea, pivoting toward my home world. The helmsman keyed in a sequence of coordinates, and the stars around us blurred into a blinding tunnel of white light as we were propelled through space at several times the speed of light.

"Blood Ruler," Koro said, sitting on my other side, "Supreme Advisor Torqa is requesting to speak with you immediately."

My ears were ringing, my brain was filled with a dull buzz, and it was taking every bit of self-control I had not to fidget in front of the crew. The thought of defending my actions to Torqa was simply more than I could bear. "Tell her I'll grant her an audience once we reach the home world. Until then, I'm not to be disturbed."

He nodded again. "Yes, sir."

I turned to look at the woman – and I was surprised to find that instead of staring at me with fear in her eyes, she was peering around the room at the control consoles. It looked as though she was trying to figure out how they worked. I couldn't help but admire that. She was able to shake off her initial panic far more quickly than most humans in her situation would have, and now she was showing genuine curiosity about the new technology that surrounded her. I may have been wrong, but it looked like she might even have comprehended some of what she was seeing.

How intelligent was she? How much could she figure out on her own about our ship's systems? I looked forward to finding out. Anyone could have a human blood slave, but one that was smart, that actively hungered for knowledge? That was a rare prize indeed.

Blood slave. Well, of course that was what she was. So why did the phrase make me so uneasy when used in this context? Why did it seem...incorrect? Inadequate, somehow, in describing her?

Could it be that I was seriously contemplating making her my mate?

I tried to banish the ridiculous notion from my mind. There had been a few isolated incidents of Valkred taking humans as mates, but it was severely frowned upon. And the idea of a Blood Ruler doing such a thing? Preposterous! How could I possibly maintain the respect of my people if I chose to share my bed – and my throne – with a member of another species...especially one as soft, weak, and easily dominated as humans? My rule would be challenged endlessly, until one of the challengers finally got lucky enough to kill me in combat and take my place.

And what would happen to her *then?*

The thought was an ugly and unthinkable one – just like the thought of anyone else drinking her blood. She had to be mine, and mine alone. I simply could not bear for it to be otherwise.

Besides, if anything, it seemed as though she was a good omen of some kind. Perhaps the Fates had allowed us to enter each other's lives as proof that negotiating a treaty with my old "friend" M'ruvev was a good idea after all.

Not that Torqa will see it that way, I thought. *One more reason to keep my advisor at arm's length, at least for now.*

The trip from Cexiea to Valkred Prime took just under three hours – but this time, it felt like years. Several times, I caught myself drumming my fingertips on the arm of my command chair, or tapping my boot nervously. Thankfully, none of the crew turned to look...but I could still tell that they noticed this behavior, and were consciously ignoring it.

No matter. The war was over at last. My bloodlust could be sated now without fear of appearing weak.

Finally, the Angel's Wrath passed all remote security clearances, entered the innermost points of the Valkred System, and settled into orbit around Valkred Prime. The human woman stared at the view screen, seeing my beautiful home world for the first time: A dark orb, swathed in a thick layer of swirling purple cloud cover.

By the stars, it was good to be back. More than that, it was good to know that my planet wouldn't be attacked by a fleet of Mana ships – that I had managed to save us from such a fate, when Torqa and my other advisors had repeatedly told me that it was impossible, that even hoping for peace was myopia and naiveté on my part.

I took her by the wrist, leading her to the docking bay where my private shuttle was housed. This time, she allowed me to pull her along without much resistance. Clearly, I was right – now that we'd made the journey, she was beginning to understand the futility of attempting to escape.

I led her onto the shuttle, and my pilot steered us out of the docking bay, bringing us down through the clouds to the continent on the western hemisphere, to the palace that had been inhabited by Valkred's Blood Rulers for millennia.

The woman gasped beside me as the sharp spires of the Ruby Stronghold came into view. They extended into the sky like the bloody claws of a demon reaching toward the heavens. The towers and parapets were carved with the crouched forms and snarling visages of the Scarlet Succubi, fiendish monsters from our most ancient legends that stole the cowardly, wicked, and unworthy from their beds and flew off with them.

The shuttle touched down in the courtyard, and my servants stepped forward to welcome me. If they were confused by the woman's presence, they were too obedient and well-trained to give any indication. I nodded to each one in turn, leading her past them to the entranceway that led to the upper chambers of the Stronghold.

She wasn't fighting me now. If anything, she seemed dazed, as though she couldn't believe her eyes.

I couldn't blame her. The first time I'd seen the Stronghold – as a small child, when my parents brought me to see it as part of a tour of the capitol city – I'd reacted in much the same way.

There were two ways up to the bedchambers on the topmost level of the castle. One was to climb the stairs, but given the fact that I was practically carrying her, that seemed unnecessarily arduous. Besides, this felt like an appropriate time to surprise her, just to keep her off-guard.

I took a deep breath and unfurled my black-feathered wings, allowing them to push through the slits concealed in the back of my tunic and spread wide. She let out a sharp yelp, her eyes practically bulging out of her head at the sight.

I smiled and nodded, glad I'd achieved the desired effect. Then I swept her up in my arms swiftly, flapping my wings and flying us to a spacious shaft with smooth walls of red marble that led directly up to the higher levels of the palace.

She clung to my neck, perhaps without even realizing it, staring down at the ground far below us in terror. I couldn't help myself – I laughed, holding her more tightly. Advanced technology was one thing, but aliens who could take flight at will were clearly outside the realm of her experience or understanding.

When we reached the ledge at the top, I nimbly touched down, still carrying her as I made my way to the spare bedchamber. Then I let her stand on her own feet again, unlocking the room and beckoning her inside.

Now was the time to talk.

"Welcome to my home," I said. "I hope you will be happy here."

She stared at me incredulously. "So you've been able to talk to me in my own language this whole time, and instead you just… what, dragged me around like some kind of fucking Neanderthal?"

"I don't know what that word means," I replied, "but considering the context you've placed it in, I can only assume you're insulting me – which is quite unwise, I might add."

"And what do you mean, 'you hope I'll be happy here?'" she continued, as though I hadn't said anything. "You *bought* me! To be your *slave!* How goddamn happy do you *think* I'm going to be about something like that, huh? How would you like it if someone did that to you? Would you be *happy*, or would you be pissed as hell?"

"I hardly think that's relevant, since we are nothing alike. Though, there are those in the galaxy who have wished to enslave me and my people, I assure you." I thought about the Mana, and felt renewed relief at the treaty we'd agreed to.

"And each time they've attempted it," I went on, "I've made sure that they've bitterly regretted it. This is a cosmos composed of predators and prey. I am a predator. Given your current status, I should think it would be fairly obvious which category you fall into."

"Oh, so 'might makes right,' is that it?" she hissed nastily. "Wow. For such a technologically advanced species, you've got the philosophies of a fucking caveman."

"I've warned you about insulting me. I won't warn you again."

"Is that right? Well, what are you going to do about it, huh? I already know you need me alive and healthy so you can drink my blood."

So, she already knew why I'd brought her here. Most impressive.

"Alive, yes," I conceded. "Healthy, certainly. But that doesn't mean I can't make your accommodations far more unpleasant. For example, I could quite easily put you in the dungeons of the Stronghold, where the other blood slaves are kept in chains. It is cold, and dark, and damp. They have no beds, no blankets, no windows to look out of. No companionship, save their wretched cellmates and the vermin that crawl and nest down there. No food, other than the vitamin paste that provides just enough nourishment and hydration to prevent them from dying. They are kept on hand to sustain my guards and servants, as you would be. Would such circumstances be more preferable to you?"

She considered this for a moment, then shook her head. "No. Sorry, but I don't buy that. You paid two hundred and fifty *thousand* rula for me… I'm not sure what a rula is exactly, but I'm damn positive that a quarter of a million of them is a lot. You didn't do that – and fly me all this way – just to toss me in the basement. You're bluffing."

I laughed, clapping my hands together. Oh, she *was* entertaining! More and more, I was glad that I'd spent so much to secure her for myself. After all, had I not ushered in a new era of peace for my people? Did I not deserve a treat for my efforts?

"You are immensely clever," I said. "Please tell me, what is your name?"

"If you must know, it's Carly. Carly Love."

"Very good. I am…"

"Akzun," she finished for me. "Blood Ruler of the Valkred. Yeah, I know. Pardon me if I don't get down on my knees and kiss your ass."

I raised an eyebrow, amused. "Then if you know who I am, you must know that I can make your stay here quite luxurious. And I intend to, as long as you keep a civil tongue in your head and show me the deference due to a man of my position. I'm eager for the pleasure of your company, but this may cease to be the case if you continue to exhibit such poor manners."

She seemed uncertain, so I went on gamely: "Think of it this way: We both know that a sharp-witted girl like you is already plotting her escape at the first opportunity. Would you rather do so from the comforts of this well-appointed chamber, or from a harsh cell with stone walls and iron bars?"

She let out a mirthless chuckle, then nodded. "Well, you've got me there. Okay…" She paused, frowning. "What am I supposed to call you? Your Highness? Your Majesty?"

"Lord Akzun should suffice," I told her. "I'm pleased that you've come to your senses. I can assure you, you won't regret it. I have other business I must attend to… please, take some time to rest, and I'll visit with you again soon."

She nodded, sitting on the edge of the bed.

I slipped out, shutting the door behind me and locking it. I had no doubt she'd try to get away – just as I was certain that she would not succeed.

Chapter Four

Akzun

I made my way down the main staircase to the parlor, knowing full well who would be waiting for me when I got there.

Sure enough, Torqa was sitting in one of the high-backed chairs upholstered with the black-and-red-striped hide of a Briziian Dusk-Mammoth – one hunted, killed, and skinned by Draavyn the First, one of Valkred's first Blood Rulers, also known as "the Black Fang." One of Torqa's long legs was slung over the armrest, and her hands were laced behind her head casually.

"An entire army of servants and bodyguards," I observed, "plus the most technologically-advanced security systems on the planet, and still, you're able to sneak into my Stronghold undetected."

She shrugged. "What kind of military and espionage advisor would I be if I weren't stealthy enough to confound such countermeasures?"

"Very well. What's so important that it couldn't wait for an official audience with me?"

"Oh, I apologize, Oh Wise and Noble Blood Ruler," she replied sarcastically, rising from the chair and giving me an exaggerated bow. "Have I disturbed you? Have I interrupted your private playtime with your lovely new toy? Please forgive me, Great Lord and Master… this humble supplicant throws herself on your mercy."

"There's no need for that tone," I reminded her through clenched teeth.

"There is if it snaps you out of the haze you've been in," she answered sharply. "First, you ignore my council regarding a treaty with those repulsive Mana, despite the number of Valkred they've butchered…"

"Negotiating peace was the surest way to prevent them from butchering more of us."

"No, *exterminating* them was the surest way!" she snapped. "The way of a warrior, a *true* Blood Ruler! Only the frightened and the feeble plead for peace; the strong *smite* their enemies, and leave their rotting corpses hanging from their battlements as a warning to any others who would take up arms against them! And then when the treaty was in front of you, you agreed to every item on it immediately, without even *attempting* to negotiate better terms for us."

"The disappearance of the Aquavor…"

"…Was a *trick,* damn it! It was *sleight of hand*, and you fell for it like a fool!"

"Commander Koro disagreed," I pointed out. "And as he is the best commanding officer in the fleet and trained to detect such illusions, I relied on his input in this matter. It was not a decision I made lightly."

"It was a decision you made *hastily*, and we both know why: You wanted to conclude the summit as quickly as possible so you could buy that human female. *Why, Akzun?* What could possibly make procuring her so important to you that you'd sweep aside all concerns for our people's well-being?"

"First of all," I began coldly, "the well-being of the Valkred is *always* my foremost priority, and I will not tolerate anyone suggesting otherwise. Second, who I choose to bring into my home is my own business, and no one else's."

"We both know that's not true. Or have you forgotten Elrisa already? She was a *traitor*, Akzun. You brought her into your home, your bed, without knowing who she really was… and as a result, our battle plans fell into the hands of the enemy, and countless lives were lost."

My spine stiffened. "That is the second time you've brought up Elrisa today, Torqa, and there will *not* be a third. I haven't forgotten her actions, and I don't intend to. But Carly is a harmless human female."

"There's no way you can be certain about that. She could have been planted in The Vein by those who wish to harm us, dosed with artificial pheromones specifically engineered to make you crave her. She could be a spy, an assassin. For all we know, she might not even really be human – she might be a Mana who's been surgically altered."

"You sound paranoid."

"I *am* paranoid, Akzun. That's my job. It's what you rely on me for. I'm no use to you otherwise."

I took a swift step forward, towering over her. "I rely on you for your counsel, and for your loyalty. That does *not* mean that I will tolerate disrespect, or implications that I am too weak or unintelligent to behave as a leader. You serve the Valkred people, Torqa, which means you serve me. If you feel that you are unwilling or unable to perform your duties without insulting me, I will be only too happy to accept your resignation. Is that understood?"

She gritted her teeth and nodded. "Yes, Blood Ruler. I serve at your pleasure, as ever."

"I'm delighted to hear it. You are dismissed. And the next time you wish to speak with me, I advise you to seek an official audience. The next time you show up in my home uninvited and unannounced, I won't hesitate to order the same punishment for you that I would for any other trespasser."

She bowed, still seething, and marched out.

I flopped down in the chair she'd previously been sitting in and sighed. By the stars, it was difficult to be a leader.

"Tell me, Akzun," Zark said jovially, stepping out from behind a nearby bookcase, "do you think Torqa is more upset that you brought a woman to your bedchamber, or that it wasn't her?"

I squeezed my eyes shut, pinching the bridge of my nose. "First her, then you. I'm starting to think I should have all of my palace guards lined up and executed for gross incompetence."

"Oh, come now," Zark said, sitting in the chair opposite mine. "You can't seriously think that those mannequins you've got patrolling the walls would be enough to stop me?"

"No, but I had some hope that the laser-webs in the hallways might," I answered wearily. "Or the tremor-detectors in the floors. Or the sentry-bots in the crawlspaces. And anyway, you don't really believe Torqa is jealous, do you?"

"Of course I do. She was jealous of Elrisa. Hell, she's jealous of me, and I'm your brother. She wants more than anything to be the most important person in your life." He paused, then added, "Well, no, that's not entirely true. She probably wants more than anything to be Blood Ruler herself, but being your consort would be a close second."

"You may be right."

"I always am," Zark said with a smirk. "But I must admit, I'm as puzzled as she is about this human female. Why did you install her in the guests' bedchamber? That's not where blood slaves are generally kept."

"The truth? I have no idea. Except that it seemed like the right thing to do. I don't know what it is about her, but she seems like more than just a blood slave to me."

Zark looked at me quizzically. "You… aren't considering her as a mate, are you?"

I didn't answer.

"Because if you are," he went on uneasily, "I'd be forced to point out that your judgment might be somewhat clouded, due to the onset of your… condition."

I slammed my fist down on the armrest. "I've had *enough* of people second-guessing my decisions and accusing me of poor judgment today! I refuse to tolerate any more, even from my brother! Our people are at peace for the first time in years, and *my bloodlust is under control!*"

"Very well, Akzun," he said quietly. "There's no need to lose your temper. I certainly didn't mean to upset you, and I apologize for doing so. I'm only looking out for your best interests and those of our people, as always."

"Torqa said essentially the same thing. Neither of you appear to have any faith in my ability to put the interests of our people first, apparently."

"I didn't mean that."

"Never mind, Zark," I snarled. "You found your way in, so you can undoubtedly find your way out."

He raised his eyebrows. "Aren't you going to give me the same threat you gave her about the next time I break into the palace?"

I curled my lip, revealing my fangs. "Would you like me to?"

He stood, leaving the room without another word.

I hung my head, massaging my temples to drive off the headache that was looming on the horizon like a thundercloud. By the stars, being a ruler was damn difficult. I brought peace to the Valkred Empire, saved thousands – perhaps even millions – of lives, and what did I get for my trouble? Snide comments, and aspersions cast on my personal choices and self-control.

Zark and Torqa. Two sides of the same coin. Both pretending to be my trusted allies while telling me to my face that I'm unworthy of the title of Blood Ruler. Damn them.

My nostrils were still filled with Carly's delicious scent; it was clinging to my clothes, and driving me mad with desire. I went to the winding stairs and began to climb them to the highest tower of the Stronghold. Flying would have been faster and easier, but I wanted an excuse to be alone with my thoughts before seeing her.

Because – even though I was loath to admit it, even to myself – what Torqa had said about Elrisa was still bothering me.

Elrisa.

She'd seemed so perfect in every way. Gorgeous, charming, intelligent, strong-willed, with a dry sense of humor that always caught me off-guard and a musical laugh that felt like blessed rain after a long drought. She was everything I'd ever searched for in a mate, and when I found her, I felt like the luckiest man in the galaxy. After only a few short weeks of courtship with her, I asked her to be my bride, and she accepted.

Zark had been happy for me, of course, if only because he loved any excuse for a party. He said he believed that such an event would be good for Valkred – a chance to acknowledge that there were still reasons to celebrate, even in the midst of a horrific war.

Naturally, Torqa had been suspicious of Elrisa from the start. I'd dismissed her concerns at the time, chalking them up to her usual paranoia and ill humor.

The wedding plans were set in motion despite Torqa's protestations, and all of Valkred rejoiced.

Then the tide of the war began to turn against us. Any time our armadas attempted to execute their missions, the Mana were there almost before we were – as though they knew what we were planning at every turn.

I'll admit, it took far too long for me to suspect that the two were related. If anything, I clung even harder to the prospect of my impending nuptials, in an attempt to escape the crippling losses suffered by our fleets. I told myself that once Elrisa and I were married, I would be stronger, more focused – that with her at my side, supporting and encouraging me every step of the way, my newfound resolve would allow me to finally win this war.

Then, a week before the wedding date, Torqa brought Elrisa before me in chains… along with irrefutable evidence that my intended had been betraying us all to the Mana since before I proposed to her.

She'd used her relationship with me to gain access to our plans, and at times, she'd even influenced my decisions regarding the war. When I demanded to know why, she threw her head back and laughed maniacally, her eyes blazing with hatred. She told me that I was the most incompetent Blood Ruler that Valkred had had in the past five centuries. She said it was time for a change, for new leadership. She confessed that K'buuda – M'ruvev's predecessor, the previous leader of the Mana – had promised the Blood Throne to *her*, if she helped him conquer us.

Naturally, I was devastated. I told Torqa to devise a fitting punishment for the traitor – any cruelty her devious mind could think up, as long as it was public and ended with Elrisa's death.

And to her credit, Torqa had done exactly that.

She'd ordered Elrisa's wings sawed off in the capitol square, then had her staked out naked under powerful ultraviolet lamps; the light blinded her, and burned her flesh. Elrisa had bled out, thirsty and starving, begging for mercy at the end, even when she knew she would receive none.

The Valkred had rejoiced in her death. But after that, I knew that their support for me – their trust in my leadership – was not what it had been. Their Blood Ruler had been duped, taken in by a pretty face, and the empire had almost been destroyed as a result. That was when I vowed I wouldn't even consider taking another mate until the war was over.

And now it was.

But…

No matter how much I wanted to shake off Torqa's concerns about Carly, I couldn't – not entirely, not after what happened before. Why *had* seeing Carly in The Vein affected me so strongly? Had the universe truly brought us together for a purpose, or was it something more insidious, something planned by my enemies, some trick of chemicals or technology to make me desire her?

Could M'ruvev be involved somehow? Was the peace summit merely a ruse to get me in the same room with Carly, to get me to let my guard down, so the Mana could eradicate us in one final, all-out assault?

I didn't want to believe any of that, but I couldn't dismiss any of it as impossible, either. The Mana were crafty, and more technologically advanced than the Valkred in many ways – that was part of what made them such formidable enemies, along with their elemental powers. Hell, for all I knew, Torqa was right, and M'ruvev *had* tricked me with some elaborate set of holograms and sensor phantoms when we were at the summit. If so, I could hardly blame him. We both wanted what was best for our people: an end to the feud.

I shook my head, trying to clear it. I could think in circles for hours, even days, but it wouldn't resolve anything. No, the only way for me to try to make sense of it all was to return to Carly's chamber and see if I could get some answers: find out who she was, and maybe even try to figure out why I'd been so instantly attracted to her.

I knew that in order to do so, I'd have to attempt to remain as objective – as suspicious, as clinically detached and observant – as possible.

I also knew how difficult that would be.

Chapter Five

Carly

I pulled the blankets from the bed around myself, shivering and rubbing my arms briskly. Christ, it was cold on this planet! And so dark! Was it like this all the time? Did the sun ever shine through the roiling purple clouds that filled the sky like a shifting pattern of bruises, or was this a land of eternal night?

The thought made me shudder. Daylight – you don't know how important it is until it's gone and you don't know if it'll ever come back.

How long would I be here, I wondered? Just what the hell happened to blood slaves in the long term, anyway? Were they eventually drained so much that they got too weak and their bodies gave out? Were they killed and dumped in a ditch when their masters got tired of them?

Well, whatever happened to them, it probably wasn't very pleasant, and I was willing to bet it certainly didn't involve letting them go on their merry way with a jaunty wave and a "live long and prosper."

I needed to get out of here. Quickly, before that intergalactic Count Chockula downstairs had a chance to sink his teeth into me.

And so what if he knew I was planning to escape? That didn't necessarily mean I'd fail.

It just meant I'd have to be smart about it.

First, I tried the door, knowing full well that it would be locked. Sure enough, the handle didn't budge. There was a locking mechanism in the metal plating that surrounded it.

Okay. Good. I could work with that.

At Cumulus, I'd taken apart and re-assembled all kinds of locks: the locks that kept the wing sections firmly in place, the locks that kept the landing gear from popping out at the wrong time, the locks on the cockpit doors – hell, even the locks on the lavatories. It didn't exactly make me an expert on picking locks, but it put me squarely ahead of most people who might find themselves in my position.

"Most people who might find themselves in my position." Right. Because suddenly, my life is a place where finding oneself as a blood slave in some gothic castle in space is totally a thing that happens. Awesome.

I felt myself starting to giggle nervously, and I stifled it. I couldn't afford to crack up now.

So. I had a lock. What I needed next were some tools.

I looked around the room. Obviously, I couldn't expect to find a fully stocked toolbox in a drawer; I'd have to improvise with whatever was on hand.

Which, as it turned out, wasn't much.

There was the bed, of course, plus a dresser, and a table and chair by the window. Escaping out the window itself was out of the question – the stained glass (depicting one of the Valkred, dressed in dark robes and hunched over a prone woman while biting her neck… which, creepy!) was sealed shut on every side, and from what I could tell, outside it was a sheer drop, straight to the ground a hundred or so feet below.

I checked the dresser drawers. They were all empty.

Shit.

Time to think outside the box, Carly, I instructed myself, surveying the room again. *That was what your supervisors at Cumulus always appreciated about you, wasn't it? The way you could come up with solutions to problems no one else could figure out? So come on, pull a miracle out of your ass like you always do. There's more than just a pat on the back and an end-of-week bonus on the line… your freedom's at stake, not to mention your life.*

"Stake." Ha. Maybe I can break off one of the chair legs, sharpen it into a stake, and drive it through his heart. That always works on vampires in the movies, right? Or hey, while I'm taking the chair apart, why not use two of the legs to make a cross? Maybe that will…

I froze.

Yes. That was it. That was *perfect.*

Not the stake or the cross, of course. Those wouldn't do any good, since I wasn't dealing with a vampire in the Earth sense of the word. No, the *chair* was the key. Because it wasn't fashioned out of some single, smooth piece of wood. Like most chairs on Earth, it was a collection of pieces (arms, legs, back) held together...by what? Nails? Screws? Bolts? Anything metal, anything that could be used on the lock?

Well, one way to find out.

I picked up the chair and smashed it against the stone floor as hard as I could, again and again, until the wood splintered and I could see the long, sharp, vaguely-grooved slivers of black metal that had been used to assemble it. Prying a couple of them loose with my bare hands wasn't easy – I got a few nasty splinters deep under my fingernails, which bled and hurt like hell – but I managed it just the same.

Great. Fantastic. Now the *real* fun could begin.

I held the slivers in my palm and bent down to examine the lock, peering into the keyhole. There wasn't much I could tell about it from the outside (God, what I wouldn't have given to have my old pen light from my tool belt so I could get a better look), but I figured no matter what planet I was on, all locks operated on the same basic principle: A metal component was moved into place so it could block the normal gears, levers, or whatever that allowed the knob to turn. Therefore, finding that component, and carefully moving it in the right direction, would be all it took to get the knob working again.

I carefully slid one of the slivers into the keyhole, feeling around with it. Sure enough, I could feel the gears that let the knob turn, and the levers that were holding them firmly. Unlike Earth locks, which mostly just relied on one blunt lever that lowered into place, this one seemed to have two sharp ones that hooked inward simultaneously.

Like Akzun's fangs, I thought, feeling goose bumps spread across my arms. It was damn hard to concentrate when all I could think about was how it would feel when those teeth plunged into my flesh like daggers, what it would be like to feel more and more of my blood pour down his throat with each hungry swallow…

Enough of that shit. Focus. You're the only one who can save yourself from that, and that won't happen if you stand here letting your own fear consume you.

Okay, so there were two levers instead of one. I'd have to feel around for both of them at once and try to lift them simultaneously. Easier said than done, but I didn't have much choice unless I wanted to be a midnight snack for my host.

There wasn't enough room for me to jigger both slivers at once unless I could bend them both, so they'd branch in separate directions when inserted. I worked on the first one, trying to bend it with my fingers and ignoring the agony that stabbed at my injured nails. It was a stubborn little sucker (but then, what did I expect from space metals?), and for a terrible second, I thought it might break before it bent. But no, it finally gave with a tiny squeal. The second sliver was a bit easier to work with – thank Christ, because I wasn't sure my fingertips could take much more.

I hooked both slivers into the keyhole, rattling them around until I found the sharp points of the levers. I tried to lift them, but the one on the left slipped immediately.

"Fuck," I murmured, inserting them again.

This time, when I pulled upward, I felt both of them start to move.

"Yes," I whispered urgently, "that's right, you bastards, just a little higher..."

Thunk. They both slipped free, falling back into place.

"Oh, you little metal motherfuckers, come on, *work* with me here," I grunted, frustrated.

The tiny fanged maw of the keyhole almost seemed to be laughing at me. In my mind, I could hear the voice of Count Von Count from the old Sesame Street show: "*Vun, two, two failed attempts at escape, ah-ah-ahhh!*"

"I'll never look at that stupid purple puppet the same way again," I growled, putting the slivers back into the hole and twisting them gently.

Click: The slivers caught the levers.

Creak: They started to lift them. "Slowly," I mumbled, "*slowly*, don't give in to the urge to rush, to push them harder out of panic, just take some deep breaths, Carly, take it nice and easy, that's right, keep your cool, or else they won't…"

Clack.

The metal panel shuddered, and I could feel the levers fall back into their recessed positions deep within the mechanism.

I grabbed the knob, and it turned easily.

"*Damn*, I'm good," I hissed triumphantly, easing the door open and peering out cautiously. I almost expected sentries to be waiting outside for me, ready to rob me of my fleeting victory.

But no, the marble hallway was empty.

Excellent.

I pressed myself flat against the cold, smooth wall, inching down the corridor like I was in some kind of spy movie. I kept waiting for some hidden door to slide open, for a legion of caped alien vampires to come swarming out at me, grabbing me, biting me – but everything remained eerily silent.

As I edged my way down the hall, I saw a doorway leading to what looked like a master bedroom. His private chamber, probably. For a brief moment, I considered searching it for anything that might prove useful – specifically, a weapon of some kind that I could use to defend myself if necessary. But that would increase the risk of him coming back and finding me. Besides, what if I did find some kind of alien laser pistol or something? Would I even know how to use it? Or would I point it in the wrong direction, hit the wrong button, and fry myself to a crisp?

No. Concentrating on finding a way out – or at least getting a solid sense of my surroundings for a later escape attempt – seemed like the best approach.

At the far end of the hall, there was an archway leading into what looked like a luxurious sitting room. It was round, and the edges of the room were bathed in total darkness. The only source of illumination was a circular beam of light coming straight down from the high ceiling, directly over a table. In the center was a bowl of what looked like it might be food, but it was hard to tell. Shiny, lumpy, colorful things that may have been fruits? Smaller dry things dusted with a sweet-smelling, powdery white substance… nuts, maybe?

My stomach growled, and I realized it had been a full day since I'd last eaten – and quite a few days since I'd consumed anything palatable. At The Vein, Nos fed the slaves a single bowl of thin, oily broth each day, with fatty bits floating on the surface. It was awful, but it was just enough to keep us from starving to death. At one point, I think Nos giggled that the herbs in it were supposed to supplement Earthling blood somehow, to make our scents and heartbeats more enticing to the Valkred customers. But with his bad English, it was hard to say for sure.

I gently picked up one of the fruits, half-expecting it to sprout sharp thorns at being touched. But no. If anything, its pleasing smell seemed to increase tenfold – like fresh Honey Crisp apples in autumn, but with faintly tropical notes, as well, that reminded me of mangoes and pineapples. Holding it close to my nose, I could almost feel a refreshing breeze in my hair.

Suddenly, Akzun's voice cut into my reverie. "You may eat them, if you wish."

I flinched, turning in the direction of the sound and staring into the gloom at the edge of the overhead light. It took a few moments for my eyes to adjust, and then I saw him: first the glimmer of his dark eyes in the shadows, and then the rest of him, sitting on a small stool and drinking a glass of red liquid.

"Why should I trust food from you?" I asked.

"Well, it's obviously not poisoned," he replied, his deep, rich voice tinged with amusement. "If I'm planning to drink your blood, I can't very well poison it first, can I? That would be suicidal, and self-destruction is hardly in my nature… no matter what my advisors might think," he added under his breath.

He spoke my language with a faint accent – I couldn't tell if he actually sounded Eastern European, or if my imagination was just playing tricks on me.

"Maybe it's something that's poisonous to my species, but not yours," I pointed out.

He shrugged. "That's a fair point. Then again, if I could drink your blood after you were dead, why wouldn't I have simply killed you by now?"

"Sadism?" I guessed.

He laughed loudly, setting his glass down on the floor and standing up. "Now you have confused me with my advisors. Torqa, anyway."

I looked at the fruit again. "So you're just trying to fatten me up first, is that it?"

Akzun shrugged mildly. "I'll admit, the foods a creature consumes can affect the way they taste. And I can only imagine that the refreshments on that table are more appealing than whatever Nos provided for you. But if you don't want them…"

I wanted to look tough in front of him, but I couldn't resist anymore – I bit into the fruit, wiping the pinkish juice from my chin. It tasted even better than it smelled, better than anything I'd ever had on Earth. Among the lower classes where I'd come from, fruits were rare, and most of them were so genetically modified and over-treated with pesticides that they had little or no taste. *Fresh* fruits were a luxury that only the upper classes could afford.

Before I knew it, I'd demolished two of the fruits and scooped a handful of the oval legumes into my mouth. They were sticky and sweet, with a delicious smoky flavor that was almost addictive.

"So what's that you're drinking?" I asked around a mouthful of food, pointing to the glass on the floor. "I'm guessing it's blood?"

A faint grimace tugged at the corners of his lips. "In a manner of speaking. It's only 'blood' in the most technical sense – my people grow it in labs for mass production and consumption. It nourishes and sustains us, and it's far easier for us to acquire and store it than to keep accumulating, feeding, housing, and harvesting blood slaves."

"Then why have blood slaves at all?"

"Because it's not the same. Ultimately, no matter how much of this artificial swill we drink, we still have a certain… hunger… that cannot be denied. Not every Valkred can afford to keep blood slaves so they can indulge in the real thing. Thankfully, as Blood Ruler of my people, I enjoy that privilege."

I thought about the fruit situation on Earth again. From the sound of things, it wasn't much different here. The poor got flavorless crap that's mass-produced from test tubes – just enough to keep them alive and working – while the rich got to enjoy tastier and more organic treats.

"How many blood slaves do you have?" I asked, picking up another fruit and taking a bite. If I was going to have my blood drained, I figured I may as well help myself to as much food as I could.

"Roughly a dozen, down in the dungeons. Enough to keep my guards and servants fed. Most of them are Mana prisoners of war. A couple of Krote as well."

"No other humans?"

He shook his head. "Members of your race are too difficult and expensive to collect in great quantities. Your blood has a peculiarly succulent flavor. Among Valkreds, it's some of the most desirable in the galaxy, second only to Lunians… and we don't interfere with them, not under any circumstances."

"Is that why you refused to wait for the auction? Why you paid so much for me?"

Akzun frowned, and I had the sense that I'd touched a nerve – that there was some other reason, one he didn't wish to share with me. One that, perhaps, he wasn't even comfortable admitting to himself.

"You ask many questions, Carly Love. I believe it is time for you to answer a few, instead. How did you come to be at The Vein?"

Now it was my turn to shrug. "Pretty standard alien abduction stuff, I guess. Walking home from my shift at the restaurant late at night, bright light in the sky, bam, whoosh, and I woke up wearing a stupid dress with this damn collar on my neck. Speaking of which, I don't suppose you could do something about that? It chafes like hell – and besides, you already bought me. You don't really need to keep the price tag on, do you?"

He took three long, gliding steps forward, hooking his thumb under the collar and pressing a hidden trigger. I was struck by how cold his fingers were, like living icicles.

"Thank you," I said quietly.

"My pleasure," he replied. "Naturally, I wish to make you as comfortable as possible. As for the dress Nos made you wear, I can't blame you for disliking it. It is rather tawdry, but then, his sort of advertising often is. What sort of raiment would you prefer?"

"Anything that's not a dress. I hate dresses. Men don't have to wear them, so why should I?"

Akzun nodded appreciatively. "I can respect that mentality, certainly. After all, the Valkred learned long ago that females are equal to males in every respect. And there are plenty of clothing styles that manage to be flattering on women without insulting or degrading them. I'm sure I can procure something you'd find more preferable."

"Again, thank you." The more time I spent with Akzun, the more unexpectedly reasonable he seemed. Charming, even, in a strange way.

"So tell me," I said, "if you were in such a hurry to drink my blood that you spent a quarter of a million space-bucks on me, why haven't you done it yet?"

Akzun seemed momentarily taken aback, as though this question had disturbed him somehow. As he opened his mouth to answer, a tall, cadaverous-looking Valkred appeared in the doorway and cleared his throat.

"Yes, Dhako, what is it?" Akzun snapped impatiently.

"My deepest apologies for intruding, Blood Ruler," Dhako said in a high, raspy voice. "But a report has just come in: The Mana flagship Aquavor was ambushed near the Stentillian Asteroid Belt. The vessel was destroyed. All aboard were killed."

Akzun's eyes widened in shock. "Was M'ruvev on the ship when it…?"

"No, Blood Ruler. He's waiting to speak with you in the screen room now." Dhako paused, then added, "The Aquavor appears to have been attacked by… by Valkred ships, sir."

"By the stars," Akzun breathed. "I'll be right there." He turned to me. "Pardon me, Carly, but this matter requires my urgent attention. Please remain here. I shall return momentarily."

And with that, he and Dhako left.

What the hell was going on?

Chapter Six

Akzun

As I marched down to the screen room, my boots clicking sharply against the marble floors, I felt like everything stable and reliable in my life was being forcibly pulled out from under me.

How could this have happened?

Could it be that a sect of my own people was so unhappy with the treaty I'd negotiated that they'd decided to break it on their own? Could my position as Blood Ruler truly be so untenable, so fragile, that any Valkred would dare to defy my will so openly? Did they *really* prefer more war and bloodshed to peace and prosperity?

I didn't know. But I knew that whatever had occurred, I'd have to root out the traitors and eliminate them fast in order to convince the Mana that I was serious about the treaty before they chose to retaliate, and to prevent additional acts of defiance that would no doubt lead to me being deposed as Blood Ruler.

After all, being deposed could only lead to two outcomes: exile… or execution. Neither seemed like an especially pleasant prospect.

The guards on either side of the screen room's entrance opened the doors, and I walked in, standing in front of the huge holo-screen. I took a deep breath and hit the button to accept the transmission.

A projection of M'ruvev's bald head immediately filled half the room. His normally bluish scales were pale pink with rage and grief. "*Akzun, what the blazing hell have you done?*"

"M'ruvev, I assure you, I'm as shocked and dismayed by this news as you are."

"Oh? Are you?" He sneered. "Did you just receive word that over three dozen of your people were incinerated in an act of base treachery and cowardice, while they were on a peaceful mission to one of your outposts? Because if not, I significantly doubt that your shock and dismay right now resemble mine in any way!"

"This attack was carried out without my knowledge."

"Damn you, Akzun, don't you see? That hardly matters! Either you're lying and you've chosen to break our treaty, or you can't control your own people! Whichever it is, you're putting me in a position of having to assume the peace we negotiated is null and void!"

"It doesn't have to be, old friend. We can still fix this. We can make peace a reality, I promise you."

"Don't you *dare* call me 'old friend,' not after this! Do you seriously believe that you're the only one dealing with factions on your own planet who didn't want this treaty? Who wanted to see this… this senseless, *interminable* war play out, until one side or the other could claim a decisive victory? I've got dissenters in my own government stirring up riots in the wake of this tragedy, saying I was weak to seek a ceasefire with you, saying that I should be replaced by a leader who won't back down until *every Valkred is enslaved or wiped out!* How do you expect me to restore order on my end? What should I tell these people? That the Blood Ruler of the Valkred sits back and shrugs while his own warriors keep murdering Mana, *and that I'm not willing to do anything about it?*"

"M'ruvev, I know you're angry, but please listen: You know me. You've known me for years. We're two of the only members of our respective empires who have taken the time to truly forge a relationship based on mutual respect and understanding —"

"More words! *Useless* words! Words won't bring back the crew of the Aquavor! I need a *solution* from you, Akzun, not a…" M'ruvev sputtered an ugly word in his native tongue that roughly translated into a subservient (and ultimately meaningless) sex act.

"I'm aware of that. But you must know I would never order or condone such an assault. Agreeing to peace, only to carry out a sneak attack? What would motivate me to behave in such a way, M'ruvev? What would it accomplish for me? All I'd have managed to do is take your flagship off the board – you still have an entire fleet that could retaliate."

"*And they will,*" M'ruvev seethed. "Make no mistake: I *did* think I knew you. I was proud to believe that you and I had managed to rise above the war our people have been waging for far too long. That day that you rescued me from the Krote pirates – I never told you this, Akzun, but at that time in my life, it was impossible for me to believe in anything good or noble in this universe. My sons had been killed in the war, my wife senselessly robbed and murdered by a narcotics dealer when she went to seek a remedy for her grief, any substance that would dull her pain. I had come to feel that there was no order, no justice, no higher purpose to be found anywhere. That for all of the technological advancements achieved by the galaxy's sentient beings, in the end, none of us would ever be more than mindless, greedy, scrabbling insects, eating and sleeping and shitting and fucking, acting purely out of self-preservation and gratification until we all inevitably died. That there was simply no meaning to anything."

He paused, wiping a tear from his bulging eye, then added in a choked voice: "I had seriously considered taking my own life that very day. Just… stepping into an airlock, hitting the release button, and swimming out as far into the cosmos as I could manage before decompression claimed me."

I was shocked to hear all of this. "M'ruvev, I had no idea."

M'ruvev shook his head. "When the Krote came for my ship, there was a part of me that welcomed them, that wanted to order the rest of the crew to the escape pods, then sit and wait to be blasted into space dust. And then you appeared on our sensor screens. At first, I thought you were some twisted final joke the stars had sent to taunt me. That you intended to watch from a safe distance, and laugh at my misfortune.

"But no. The Angel's Wrath incinerated two of the raiders' ships, and drove the third away. You called out to us. Made sure we were safe. You even offered emergency supplies and medical aid. When you left, I wasn't foolish enough to think that such a small, isolated incident would end the hostilities between the Valkred and the Mana. But it restored my hope that such a thing *could* be possible, in time. More than that – it made me feel that there *was* selflessness and nobility out there. That the universe was not entirely cold and indifferent. I petitioned my predecessor K'buuda to seek out peace, and when he was no longer in charge, I did everything I could to replace him. All so we could reach this point. So we could end this destructive conflict once and for all."

His lip curled, baring his small rows of teeth. When he spoke again, his voice cracked. *"And now you have ruined it all.* Why? I don't know. Maybe your advisors somehow convinced you that you'd conceded to the terms too easily, or that the disappearance of my ship was some sort of elaborate illusion. Whatever the reason, whatever your excuse… the peace we agreed to was a beautiful, fragile thing, and *you have shattered it beyond repair."*

"I don't believe that," I interjected quickly. "And what's more, M'ruvev, I don't think you want to believe that either. You said it yourself – there are elements within your government that don't want the treaty to succeed. I have the same problem among my own people. Surely, this attack on the Aquavor was carried out by individuals who wish to prolong the war. What information can you send us about the Valkred ships that attacked your people? Design configurations, identification codes, even engine output readings?"

M'ruvev sighed. "This data was masked with static sensor fields, holographic projections, and obscured engine signatures."

"There! You see?" I crowed triumphantly. "If I truly wanted to keep waging war on your people, why would I conceal such things while still allowing you to determine that the ships firing on you were from the Valkred fleet? No, those ships were being flown by crew members who weren't supposed to be piloting them. The masked data was for my benefit as much as yours, I assure you. Whoever did this was acting independently."

"As I've said, Akzun, it *doesn't matter."* M'ruvev groaned, frustrated. "To the Mana, all that matters is that you can't keep your own forces in line, which is still a solid argument for us to resume the war and take your empire over for ourselves."

"Then give me a chance to *get* my forces in line!" I pounded my fist on the control panel, and the image of M'ruvev fizzled briefly. I took a deep breath, trying to calm myself. "You allowed me to restore your faith in the galaxy once, old friend. Give me a chance to do that for you again. Allow me to find the ones responsible for this and deal with them. Don't let our shared dream of peace die with those poor souls on your flagship."

M'ruvev considered this carefully, then gave me an almost imperceptible nod. "Very well. You have five days, Akzun. That's as long as I can give you before I must heed the will of my people and rededicate our resources to the swift and decisive conquest of Valkred. I beg you: Do *not* make me regret this reprieve."

M'ruvev's holographic form vanished.

I sighed angrily. All those overtures leading up to the summit, and it felt like we were right back where we started. Worse – now that M'ruvev felt personally betrayed, he wouldn't hold back one bit. He'd keep coming and coming until one of us was dead and the other victorious.

And now I had to deal with *another* traitor among my own people.

I touched a comm button. "Send for Torqa and Zark. I must speak with them immediately."

Dhako's voice replied, "They're already here, Blood Ruler. They heard about the attack on the Aquavor, and they're waiting to see you."

"Good. Send them in."

As I waited for them to enter, I thought about the haunted look in M'ruvev's eyes as he talked about the day I rescued his ship – a look that was all the more chilling, given how expressionless most Mana's faces are. They were, by and large, known as a stoic people, and have long endured many racist jokes from other species about being "cold fish."

I'd always felt that M'ruvev was a bit more sensitive than the rest of the Mana, based on my dealings with him. But I'd never had any inkling of his deeply-rooted mental and emotional issues before. If I'd known about them previously, would I have used them as a way to find common ground with him – or would I have tried to determine some way to exploit them, to turn the tide of the war in my favor?

I wanted to believe it was the former, but deeper down, I suspected that if it had come down to it, it might have been the latter instead. War doesn't often give us a chance to explore the better aspects of our nature, does it?

The door to the screen room swished open, and Zark entered, with Torqa right behind him. Both wore expressions of concern.

"I am so sorry this has transpired, Blood Ruler," Torqa said, putting a hand on my shoulder. Her face was still stern, but this was the most genuine sympathy I'd ever heard in her voice. "I know how hard you've worked for this peace treaty, how much you wanted to believe in its outcome."

"Even as you openly criticized me for signing it," I reminded her, "and called my leadership into question."

Her gaze never wavered. "I provided the best counsel I could, as I always have and always will. Still, I would never wish such a disappointment on you. I take no pleasure in having been right."

"*Were* you right, Torqa?" Zark asked, a bit sharply. "Were you really? From what we've been able to determine, it was the Valkred who broke the treaty, not the Mana."

"Which only proves my point, Zark," she replied evenly. "Our own people weren't ready to see you capitulate to these aliens. They were so shamed by this act of appeasement, they chose to move on their own. The way to keep them under control would have been to refuse to back down until we had accepted the Mana's unconditional surrender."

"So that's your theory." I turned to Zark. "What's yours, brother?"

Zark shrugged. "It's hard to deny the evidence pointing to hardline elements in the Valkred military. Still…"

"What?" I demanded impatiently. "We're in the middle of a crisis, Zark. We don't have time for dramatic pauses and pensive chin-stroking."

"Well, I only mean to say: how many of our vessels were captured by the Mana during the course of the war? Plenty of their own people disapproved of the peace summit. They might have reconfigured our own ships, updated them to camouflage the sensor readings, and fired on their own people. Depending on their level of zealotry, it's a sacrifice I'm sure they'd be willing to make, just to keep the flames of war stoked."

"I'm still not convinced that the human female isn't involved in this somehow." Torqa sneered. "She shows up in the same room where the summit is being held, and suddenly you just *have* to possess her, outside the bounds of all reason or sense? And then, her first evening here, there's a skirmish that threatens the peace? No, no, this is all *far* too coincidental. I still maintain that she was sent to you deliberately, to distract and disarm you at the exact moment when it's *most important* for you to focus on your duties as Blood Ruler."

"Presuming that your far-fetched theory is true – and I highly doubt that it is – who sent her?" Zark asked. "The Mana? Our own people? For all we know, it could even be some third group… maybe the Krote wanted to destabilize the peace so we'd be too busy fighting each other to defend ourselves from their raiding parties. Or some other species, worried that a long-term alliance would threaten their trading interests."

"Congratulations, both of you," I said dourly. "You've managed to narrow the list of potential suspects down to every civilized race in the galaxy. Wonderful. At this rate, the five days M'ruvev gave us to get to the bottom of this will be just enough time for everyone on our planet to write out their Last Will and Testament."

"If we only have five days, then we must act fast," Torqa insisted. "Blood Ruler, you *must* allow me to properly interrogate the human woman, to make sure she's not a factor in all of this."

"I'll handle the woman myself," I replied.

Torqa rolled her eyes. "Imagine my surprise."

"I won't have you torture her to death on the basis of a mere theory – and a flimsy one, at that. No, Torqa, if she's hiding something from us, I'll discover it, I assure you. Meanwhile, you will pursue any leads pointing to our own forces' participation in this attack, and Zark will make inquiries among the Mana."

"Why is Zark assigned to the Mana?" she balked, putting her hands on her hips.

"Because I have more finesse, of course," Zark answered her with a grin. "If you go charging in headfirst and guns blazing, the Mana's mouths will snap shut, and the tensions will only be escalated. But as Akzun's beloved brother, I can make better inroads, since they'll assume I'm as sympathetic to the cause of peace as our Blood Ruler is."

I nodded. "Precisely. Now get to it, both of you, and tell me what you find. We don't have any time to waste."

Torqa saluted, turning on her heel and leaving. Zark stayed an extra moment, giving me a rueful smile and a small nod of understanding before he left. He knew how depressing the news of the Aquavor must have been for me.

I considered returning to Carly – but I was too emotional, too filled with rage and confusion. I was worried that if I were in her presence, these things would overtake me, and I'd give in to my desire to drink from her. And I worried even more that if I did drink from her, I wouldn't be able to stop myself until it was too late, until I'd consumed too much of her blood and inadvertently killed her.

No. That would be an expensive mistake.

But some part of me knew the expense was the least of my worries. That I simply didn't wish to harm her.

I needed to exorcise these feelings before seeing her again.

First, though…

I hit the comm button. "Dhako?"

"Yes, sir?"

I keyed a sequence into the console. "I'm sending you some design specifications. Would you see to it that they are assembled immediately and delivered to the human upstairs?"

"Of course, sir. Right away."

"Good. Thank you."

I stepped out of the screen room and headed toward the training chamber, to lift weights and leap catwalks and dodge automated spiked weapons until the more immediate effects of the bloodlust had been sweated away.

I prayed to the Succubi that it would be enough.

Chapter Seven

Carly

While Akzun was away doing… well, whatever it was that Blood Rulers did when they were summoned for emergencies… I wandered around the tower a bit, exploring. I was trying to find out as much as I could about my host. My anxiety regarding my situation had started to subside during our last conversation, and had been replaced with a ravenous curiosity.

My entire life, I'd never known that there was intelligent life on other planets. Now I'd learned that not only did aliens exist, but some of them were vampires! Who would have guessed that? I was eager to learn more.

I found the strange blend of futurism and gothic architecture particularly fascinating. Clearly, the Valkred were a race that embraced new technologies while still managing to respect and appreciate the beautiful elements of their low-tech past. I felt like humans could take a lesson from them in that regard; on Earth, everyone was obsessed with erasing the lovely edifices and antique masterworks of bygone eras in favor of whatever was newer, shinier, and cheaper. True craftsmanship was rare, and only found in the upper classes as hobbies and keepsakes. Everyone else had homes, clothes, furniture, and appliances that were mass-produced and only meant to last a handful of years at most.

There was no doubt that this planet was a bizarre and unfamiliar place – yet in some ways, I almost felt more at home here than I had on my own world.

After all, had it ever even *been* "my world?" As a member of the poorer class, I'd gone through most of my life feeling like a tenant, and an unwelcome one at that. I'd never really owned much of anything. The clothes I wore were secondhand. The places I lived belonged to landlords who had more money than I'd ever see in my lifetime. No matter how hard I worked, I could be fired on a whim.

Here, at least, I was important to someone.

I was still wishing Akzun had answered my question earlier. If he was so thirsty for me, why hadn't he drank any of my blood yet? Could it be that he was worried about scaring or hurting me? If so, a quarter of a million rula was a lot to pay just to keep me around as a decoration.

He couldn't have… *feelings* for me… could he?

I had to admit, the more time I spent with him (and the more my fear faded), the more handsome and graceful I was starting to find him. The pointed, vaguely wolf-like shape of his face was compelling, his dark eyes were hypnotic, and his pale skin made him look like a marble statue come to life. And those amazing feathered wings! When he'd flown me up to the top floor of the castle, I'd been too upset and indignant to enjoy it. Now, there was a part of me that was eager for him to sweep me up and fly me around again.

Jesus, what a surreal experience. Is this what my life has become – some silly B-movie from the 1950s? *I Married An Alien From Outer Space*?

The thought made me giggle. Then I heard someone clear his throat behind me, and turned to find the one called Dhako standing a short distance away, holding a square, flat box.

"For you," he said. His accent was much heavier than Akzun's. "From the Blood Ruler."

"Thank you," I said, taking the box from him.

He nodded, turned, and walked away.

I opened the box, and my jaw dropped. Inside was a form-fitting, long-sleeved shirt of silky, shimmering fabric that rippled in various shades of cool blue, like an ocean – and matching pants that were cut more loosely, with a high waist and tapered legs. Underneath were low-heeled black boots that came up just above the ankle.

Speaking of craftsmanship, these clothes were magnificent.

And he remembered that I prefer pants to dresses. How considerate of him.

I ducked into Akzun's bedchamber, slipping out of the atrocious dress Nos had forced me to wear and putting on the outfit my host had sent me. As I dressed myself, I looked at the rows of portraits hanging on the walls. They were incredibly detailed renderings of proud, fierce-looking Valkred men and women.

Members of his family, perhaps? Or previous Blood Rulers? I made a mental note to ask him about it when he returned.

Meanwhile, there was a full-length mirror in the corner, and I twirled in front of it, admiring my new look.

Guess vampires are fine with mirrors after all… in space, at least.

The clothes were gorgeous. More than that, they almost seemed alive – I could feel the smooth fibers expanding and contracting against my skin, and warming me (which was good, since apparently these Valkreds liked to keep their homes like refrigerators). Part of me felt like I should be uneasy about clothing that breathed on its own, but the exquisite softness made it impossible for me to worry.

Maybe that's part of what they're designed to do. Maybe they're supposed to keep blood slaves calm so they won't try to run or put up a fight when it's time for their owners to snack on them.

Well, if that was true, I didn't much care. Calm was good. Calm meant it would be easier for me to consider my present situation, and what – if anything – I should do about it.

"So," a female voice behind me snapped, "it appears as though you're just like the other females of your species: materialistic and vain. Not that you have much to be vain about, mind you."

I turned and saw the Valkred woman who had been with Akzun at The Vein, sneering at me coldly.

"Short and squat," she continued, walking around me in a tight circle and sizing me up. "Weak, brittle, mewling creatures, with ugly pinkish skin and flat little teeth. The only appealing thing about you is the blood you carry around inside you, and even that is too cloying and sugary – just thinking about it makes my fangs ache. Still, I suppose it's our leader's prerogative to indulge in expensive sweets now and then. Frankly, though, I don't know why he doesn't just drain you and get it over with."

"If I've done something to offend you," I began hesitantly, "I certainly didn't mean to, and I apologize. As you've probably guessed, I'm new to this planet, and I'm unfamiliar with your customs –"

"Then again," she went on as though I hadn't spoken at all, "he wouldn't be the first Blood Ruler to 'play with his food,' as you Earthlings say." She gestured to one of the paintings. "Vylaad the Tenth, for example, was fond of making his slaves watch as he drained their blood into a series of decorative glass bottles, leaving just enough inside them to remain alive so that he could wait for them to produce more red cells to do it all over again." She pointed to another face on the wall. "Then there was Batreyia the Fourth. She preferred to attach Gorvyan leeches to her slaves and let them gorge until they were fat and succulent enough to be removed, roasted, and eaten as a delicacy. Something about the way their digestive enzymes interacted with the blood made the flavor more appealing to her… and she claimed that the screams of horror from the slaves were her favorite music to dine to."

"Listen, lady, if you're trying to scare me…"

"I am, and I'm succeeding. You may posture all you wish, but I can hear your pulse quicken from across the room, and it doesn't lie." She singled out another portrait. "Then, of course, there was Rennfil the Seventh, a personal favorite of mine. He enjoyed feeding pieces of his blood slaves to each other, letting their unique tastes mingle… and savoring the terror in their eyes as they were forced to chew and swallow their companions' body parts and organs raw. *'Have you done something to offend me,'* you ask? Your very *presence* here is an offense to me."

"I'm sorry to hear that, but in case you haven't noticed, coming here wasn't exactly my choice," I snapped. Whoever this woman was, she was pissing me off.

She raised an eyebrow. "Wasn't it? Somehow, I doubt that." She sniffed in my direction, and her nose wrinkled. "Hmm. Your scent isn't attractive to me, so obviously, your pores were engineered to secrete pheromones specifically targeting Akzun. Impressive. You'll have to tell me how your people managed that – after you've told me who sent you, and the parameters of your mission."

"My… mission?" I asked, confused. "I don't…"

She took an ominous step toward me, towering over me easily. "Don't waste my time with denials and falsehoods, you filthy little spy. Who do you report to? The Mana? The Krote? Some other race? Are you even really human, or were you simply altered to look, sound, and smell like one? If you tell me now, I can promise that your lifelong incarceration will be served in relatively comfortable conditions to reflect your cooperation. If you continue to hide your true purpose here, however, you will be tortured at great length, you *will* eventually talk, and death will be the only reward left for me to offer you."

Suddenly, a horrible pain flared through my head, sharp enough to make me cry out and press my fingertips to my temples. It was like nothing I'd ever felt before. Not just agony, but a strange pushing and tearing sensation – as though hands wrapped in rusty barbed wire were rummaging around roughly in my brain, ripping it apart, looking for something buried inside.

She smirked, her eyes never leaving mine. Her lips didn't move, but somehow, I could hear her voice in my head: ***Your mental defenses are more impressive than I'd have given you credit for. One more piece of evidence to convince me you're not really an Earthling. But no matter who you are or where you came from, it's a grave mistake to believe you can keep your secrets from me for long.***

The pain was becoming excruciating, unbearable. The room span around me, and I felt a thin trickle of blood from my nose…

"*Torqa, that's enough!*"

We both turned to the doorway, where Akzun stood with his arms folded.

"It will be *enough*," the one called Torqa snarled, "when she *tells me what I need to know*."

"I told you that Carly would be my responsibility, not yours. I believe I was quite clear about that, just as I was clear in assigning you to root out any traitors within our own ranks. Now get to it, Torqa, before your unwillingness to follow orders costs you your position… or worse."

Torqa drew herself up to her full height and stomped out of the room.

I let out a sigh of relief, and Akzun entered, looking me over admiringly. "You look ravishing, Carly. Are the clothes acceptable to you?"

"Yes, thank you. Who was that?"

"Torqa is my Supreme Advisor."

"Yeah? So what's her problem with me?" I asked. "What did I ever do to her?"

He gave me an embarrassed smile. "Not a thing, I'm sure. We're simply having a difference of opinion these days, she and I. The dreary realities of politics, I'm afraid. Nothing to concern yourself with. She wouldn't dare harm you, no matter what she said."

"Well, that's good to know, at least."

I turned to look out the window. Far below us, there were colorful city lights shining and twinkling. If I listened closely enough, I could even hear faint echoes of exotic music, what sounded like delicate flutes and pattering drum beats.

"Your planet's pretty at night," I said.

Akzun smiled. "Then it's a good thing our nights tend to last eighteen hours. As lovely as it appears from up here, I can assure you it's even more captivating when observed at the ground level. Perhaps you will allow me to show you around?"

"Sure, why not?" I was trying to sound breezy, but the exchange with Torqa had left me extremely unsettled. He said she wouldn't hurt me.

I wasn't so sure.

Chapter Eight

Akzun

Less than an hour later, Carly and I were strolling through Kor Püskla, the capitol city of Valkred. A battalion of bodyguards walked in perfect formation around us, their ceremonial spears held high, their telepathy-dampening helmets fixed tightly to their brows, and their expressions unreadable.

Are they content to carry out the task at hand? Are they loyal? Do they still trust in the wisdom and leadership of their Blood Ruler? Or are they filled with resentment at having to watch me and guard me while I entertain a human whose official status is "blood slave?" Are the men and women charged with protecting me the same ones who were involved in the betrayal of the treaty and the destruction of the Aquavor?

More than anything, I wanted to believe in Torqa's ability to find the traitors hiding in our ranks and bring them to justice. But how could I, when she was so fixated on Carly instead?

Meanwhile, Carly walked arm in arm with me, taking in the sights. She looked impressed, which pleased me immensely. It was almost as though I was enjoying Kor Püskla anew through her eyes: the chains of glowing red lanterns strung between the buildings' doorways, the rich smells and sizzles of vendors grilling skewers of rapta meat and sugared vespis blooms, the folk songs and lively tunes of the street musicians, the Ven'Truu dancers spinning and leaping as the crowd applauded.

How I wanted her. It was all I could do to keep from staring at the throbbing arteries in her neck and licking my lips – I didn't want to frighten her. Even so, just being so close to her was driving me mad with desire. But was it for her blood… or for something more?

I still couldn't be sure.

"This place is so beautiful," Carly said, awestruck.

"I'm delighted to hear that you think so."

"I guess before we left the castle, you had your guards clear away all the poor and homeless from the streets for my benefit, huh?"

I raised an eyebrow. "Certainly not. What you see on these streets now is exactly what you'd see here at any other time, I can assure you. Valkred is entirely free of poverty and homelessness. Our people occupy various social and economic statuses, naturally, based on the careers and lifestyles they choose to pursue. But here on my home world, no one who is willing to contribute to our society ever goes without food and the artificial blood they need to sustain themselves. No one is ever without a roof over their heads, or clothes to protect themselves from the elements. No illness goes untreated. As Blood Ruler, my primary objective – other than protecting the Valkred from those who would do us harm – is to ensure that every citizen is well taken care of, with no exceptions. It's a duty I take seriously. And, I might add, a fairly easy thing to implement and maintain."

Carly let out a humorless chuckle. "Yeah, says you. On Earth, it seems pretty goddamn impossible. My world is full of people whose needs are ignored by those in power, who scrape and starve and struggle every day just to survive."

"Yes, I know all about the way things are done on Earth," I said. "The obstacle to this way of life on your planet, Carly, is that those in power have no desire whatsoever to see it put into practice. They could easily eliminate all hunger and poverty without any real sacrifice to their own luxury and comfort. They simply *choose not to*. Because in the end, the rich who rule your world do not count their wealth in terms of how much money and property they have, but *how little others have by comparison*. That thrill, that rush of superiority, is so paramount to them that they cling to it beyond all reason. Their lack of compassion or empathy makes them feel powerful. Their ability to sneer at those with less, to pity them, or to ignore them completely is an addiction… one they've always been in the grip of, one they have no intention of overcoming."

Carly's eyes widened. "You know a lot about where I come from. Is that why you know English? Do all the other members of the Valkred speak English, too?"

"No, not all. In fact, among my people, it's quite rare. Torqa and my brother Zark can speak it, as well as some of my guards, only because their job is to advise and protect me. The Valkred's dealings with Earthlings have been limited, for the most part, but it's a necessity for those in my position to understand the languages of all we have diplomatic relations with."

"Whoa, whoa, hang on: *Diplomatic relations?* You mean to tell me that you've visited our planet, you've got an official relationship with the people who run it – and I had to find out aliens existed by being fucking *abducted* by one? How can that be possible? How could they keep a secret like that from most of the people on Earth? Why would they? And for that matter, with so many extraterrestrial empires armed with, I don't know, laser blasters and ships that can travel faster than light, how come none of you have ever just gone ahead and colonized us?"

I laughed. "Once again, so many questions. The simple answer is this: Long ago, the most powerful empires in the galaxy learned of the existence of Earth, and vice versa. We suspected that any attempt to conquer your world would be a difficult and costly endeavor… and more than that, we did not relish the idea of fighting amongst ourselves for such a negligible prize, especially since you humans had already managed to poison and destroy so many of your natural resources. As a result, we came to a sort of understanding – an accord, signed and agreed upon by all of our worlds. We would not invade your planet, we would keep our existence a secret from your lower economic classes, and in exchange, we were granted permission to periodically poach members of those classes to be used as slaves."

"So what you're saying is, our leaders totally sold out us poor people in order to stay on your good side?" Carly sighed. "Screwed over by the super-rich once again. Why am I surprised? Well, no, I guess it's a *little* surprising, given that you just told me how proud you are of eradicating this sort of inequality on your own world… yet here you are, perpetuating that same system on ours. Kind of hypocritical, don't you think?"

I raised my eyebrows. "It is not for us to fly around the galaxy imposing our own systems of governance on other species."

"No, you just scoop up a handful of them now and then and make them your slaves."

"You… have a point," I conceded. "There are many men like Nos in the Valkred Empire, whose businesses rely almost entirely on slaves. I might not approve of it, but if I attempted to dismantle that entire industry, I'd be risking a revolt."

"So instead, you support the industry by dropping a quarter of a million rula in Nos's pocket."

"I had to," I said through clenched teeth. Her sharp mind and strong will were exhilarating. More than that, her scent was tickling the back of my throat, driving me insane with passion. It took all of my self-control not to drink her blood right here in the street. "I had no choice. Now perhaps it might be best if you changed the subject."

"Okay," she replied gamely. "Tell me this, then: If your people are so into the concept of minding your own business, then what's the deal with the Mana? Are they those fish-looking guys you were talking to in the bar before you bought me?"

"Yes."

"And based on what Torqa said earlier, I'm assuming you're at war with them?"

"We were. I suppose, for the moment, we still are."

"Why? What is it you're fighting about?"

I took a deep breath, thinking of the best way to explain. "Centuries ago, races like mine and the Mana were far more warlike, concerned with endless expansion, subjugating other species and claiming their resources as our own. That was how our empires were initially forged. Then, Kochak the Second – the previous Blood Ruler – ascended to the throne. He inspired the Valkred to evolve beyond our desire for battle and conquest. To concentrate on improving upon what we had already built, rather than simply thirsting for more. We embraced peace, and for over three hundred years, the Valkred Empire was a paradise."

I paused. The memory of the former Blood Ruler was still a difficult one for me.

"Kochak was… a mentor to me, especially after my father died," I went on. "More than anyone, he molded me into the man I am today. I served him faithfully for half a century as his trusted guard and advisor, just as Torqa serves me now. When he passed away, I was chosen to ascend to the throne in order to continue his good works. And I tried. By the *stars*, I tried. Unfortunately, during that time, the leader of the Mana was a brutish warlord named K'buuda. He decided that his people could not prosper in peace – that the only way to thrive, to keep his people united, was to return to the old ways of expansion and conquest. I suppose we seemed like the easiest target for them. So we went back to war, this time in the name of self-preservation."

Carly appeared to be thinking this over carefully. "So that day in the bar, you were trying to negotiate a treaty with them, is that it? And now some of your ships have blown up one of theirs, and the war's back on?"

I nodded.

"I'm so sorry," she said. "And I'm sorry about your father. Mine's dead, too; he had a heart attack when I was just a kid. I didn't have a mentor to look up to after that, but I can only imagine losing Kochak would have been almost as hard for you."

Before I could respond, one of the Valkred in the crowd around us drew closer – for a moment, it looked like he was going to try to get past the barricade of guards. Instead, he flung words over their shoulders. "Hey, Akzun! What kind of weak-blooded coward tries to bargain for peace with those slimy, stinking fish-people after everything they've done to us, huh? You're a disgrace!"

An older Valkred woman pressed in from the other side, so close I could smell the sour tang of her breath. "*I'll* tell you what's disgraceful!" she croaked. "Agreeing to a treaty, and then breaking it within a day! A *true* Blood Ruler would have waged war openly, instead of relying on subterfuge. We're ashamed of you, Akzun!"

I tried not to let my apprehension show, but when I stole a glance at Carly, she was pale and her eyes were wide. I put a hand on her upper arm to comfort her.

"Look at him!" an adolescent Valkred called out mockingly. "Strutting around the city and feeling up some human blood slave instead of figuring out a way to win this war! Mark my words, Akzun will get us all killed!"

"Oh, how I long for the days of Vylaad and Rennfil!" a wizened old crone screeched from the crowd. "At least they knew how to protect us from our enemies. Let a *real* warrior sit on the throne, Akzun! Step down! Step down!"

The crowd began to echo her, chanting *step down* over and over, their voices deafening.

"We should go, I think," I announced to the guards. They rearranged their configuration, facing the palace and marching us toward it.

Someone threw a rock.

One of the guards moved to intercept it, and it hit the armor plate on her shoulder, bouncing off harmlessly.

Then came another, larger one.

This time, it hit a guard in the helmet with surprising force. The guard recoiled slightly, and I could see that some of the anti-telepathy circuitry in his helmet was exposed. Blue sparks hummed and crackled inside.

It wasn't much of a crack in the overall defenses surrounding us, but it was still enough for a trickle of our attackers' hostile thoughts to get through, their jeers and threats reverberating in my head.

N*ot good enough…*

Not a real leader, just a pathetic, spineless fool…

My wife, my CHILDREN, the Mana will make them slaves, and it's ALL YOUR FAULT, Akzun…

Should be executed in the public square, to make room for a TRUE BLOOD RULER…

I looked at Carly, and saw that she was experiencing the same psychic assault. Her eyes were squeezed shut, and she was gripping the sides of her head as though she were worried her skull would fly apart.

"Blood Ruler?" the lead guard asked. "Should we use force to quell this disturbance?"

"No," I answered immediately. The last thing I needed was to further fuel their rage. "Just get us home as quickly as possible."

The guards escorted us the rest of the way, shielding us from stones, bottles, and other thrown objects until we reached the doors of the castle. I dismissed them once the doors shut behind us, then turned to Carly.

"I'm so sorry you had to witness such an unfortunate display," I said sadly. "This was not how I had hoped we'd spend our evening together. Would you like me to fly you up to your bedchamber?"

"Thanks for asking this time, instead of just grabbing me," she replied. She was trying to sound flippant, but I could hear the faint quivering in her voice. "Yes, I'd like that, thank you."

I picked her up tenderly, unfurling my wings and flying us up to the highest tower. Instead of setting her down when we reached the platform, I carried her the rest of the way to her bed and placed her in it gently. She didn't seem to mind.

"Tell me," she said quietly, "are all the members of your race able to… you know, read minds? Communicate telepathically, like Torqa and the others did?"

I nodded slowly.

"And do you suspect I'm some kind of spy, like she does?"

I chuckled. "If I say yes, I'll be lying. If I say no, you'll think I'm a fool and an unfit leader, due to my lack of caution."

"Well, I mean, if you really want to know for sure, why don't you just read my mind and find out for yourself?"

"Doing such a thing without so much as a by-your-leave seemed impolite."

She sat up in bed, putting her hand over mine. The feeling sent tingles all through my body. "I'm giving you permission. I won't fight it. I'll open my mind up to you, and you can find out whatever you need to."

"Very well," I said, concentrating.

Valkred telepathy can be a one-way process, when we're seeking specific information in the mind we're reaching out to. However, there's also a somewhat invasive quality to that method, which many find disconcerting.

So instead, I opened my mind to her as well.

I told myself it was simply to put her more at ease, so I could find what I needed to more efficiently. I told myself that since she herself was not a natural telepath, it didn't matter that I'd opened the door to my own thoughts – she wouldn't know how to walk through them, how to gather any information from my brain.

But…

"… But that's not really it, is it?" Carly asked breathlessly, her brown eyes never leaving mine. "You *want* to open your mind to me. You *want* me to know what you're thinking and feeling, so you won't have to say it out loud. Because… " She paused, and her eyebrows shot up in surprise. "Because I'm not just a slave to you, am I? No, you see me as a… mate?"

This revelation made me hesitant to proceed further. I hadn't even wanted to admit those things to myself, let alone her. I was tempted to end the mental connection, to slam the door shut and hurry out of the room now that my true intentions had been discovered.

Instead, I pushed a bit deeper into her thoughts, trying to find any evidence that she wasn't who she said she was, that Torqa might be right about her.

"That's right," she whispered. "Go in as far as you need to."

There was nothing there. According to her thoughts, her memories, Carly was exactly who she appeared to be.

And she desired me almost as much as I did her.

She touched my face lightly, stroking my cheek. "I had no idea how complicated your life is," she said. "Or how lonely."

I leaned in and our lips met – softly at first, our passion building swiftly, like a fire blazing out of control.

One that would consume us both.

Chapter Nine

Carly

Akzun took me in his arms, kissing me and holding me tight. As my tongue explored his, I could feel the pointed tips of his teeth. There was something sexy about having those dangerous fangs pressed against my mouth and knowing that he wasn't going to use them to hurt me.

Am I really going to do this? Make love to some alien ruler on a distant world, when he bought me as a slave? Christ, how bizarre has my life become?

I heard his voice in my brain: ***If you don't want to…***

No, I do, I do! I insisted. *It's just… wow, you know?*

Yes. I know.

I reached around behind his back, touching his feathered wings and feeling him tremble with desire. He pressed himself closer to me, and his heartbeat thrummed next to mine – it was so powerful. I wondered if Valkred hearts were larger because of the blood they consumed.

Our minds were still connected. The sensation was unlike anything I'd ever experienced: an entirely different set of thoughts and feelings echoing just behind mine, whispering, reverberating. I could almost *see* his lust for me, expanding inside him like a snake uncoiling and preparing to strike.

"Are you going to bite me, Akzun?" I asked, with both my lips and my mind.

No, he intoned inside my head. ***Not tonight.***

"Why not?"

For the first time since our minds joined, I felt him hastily withdraw a specific set of thoughts from me – as though he'd suddenly dropped a dark curtain over them, concerned by what I might see. Instead, he kissed me more fervently.

What are you afraid of? I wondered.

His response was a reflex, the words erased as quickly as they were spelled out, too fast for me to read.

I fear nothing. I want you. Give yourself to me, Carly. Now.

I didn't bother with thinking or speaking words – just an image of a door opening to signify that I was entirely his, that he was welcome to enter me on any level he wished.

He pulled my shirt up over my head in a single smooth motion and gently pushed me back down on the bed. I kicked my boots off, then slid out of my pants, revealing my naked body to him.

You are utterly breathtaking, he sighed within my thoughts. His eyes made the air between us feel magnetic. I could practically hear it hum.

My anticipation was burning in my core. I wanted him on top of me, inside me.

And he knew it.

He shrugged his tunic off and undid his trousers, lowering himself over me. His cold fingers slipped between my legs, finding the folds of my wet pussy and making them tingle. I gasped at his touch, but the chill of his skin was oddly refreshing once I adjusted to it.

Do you like my touch? he asked.

"Oh, God, yes," I whispered. "Please don't stop."

The tip of his middle finger pressed against my clit – gently at first, then firmly, insistently. I arched my neck and moaned loudly. It felt like currents of electricity were traveling from the surface of my skin all the way into the base of my spine, the voltage increasing steadily, the jolts coming faster, faster, until I wasn't sure I could take it any more.

There were beads of sweat on my forehead, my upper lip, my chest. Droplets of my own moisture trickled down my inner thighs, pooling beneath my hips.

But Akzun was still calm and cool and dry. Once again, I thought of some gorgeous marble statue come to life.

"Take me, Akzun," I begged. "I need to feel you."

Then feel me you shall.

Akzun withdrew his hand and held my wrists down on the bedspread. He used a knee to spread my legs wider, and suddenly, I felt his cock; it was stiff against my labia, quivering gently, as icy and powerful as every other part of his body.

There was a push, my lips parted, and then he was deep inside of me. I cried out sharply, every muscle tensing from head to toe. I tried to lift my body to take him into me even more deeply, but he kept me pinned down. His thoughts told me that this was going to be on *his* terms… that he was going to have me *his* way, or not at all.

I took a deep breath and surrendered to him, body and soul.

His first thrusts were almost painfully slow. With my mind, I begged him to go faster, harder, knowing he could hear me, knowing that he wouldn't care – that he would do as he pleased with me, that he savored my want, my need for him.

The top of his shaft rubbed hard against my clit with every plunge into me, the tip pressing insistently against my innermost walls, my most private places.

"Oh Akzun," I cried out, "Oh God, you feel so *good*…"

His face was inches away from mine; his eyes were locked on the side of my neck, his mouth open, his fangs shining in the gloom of the chamber. He was panting hard, and as he licked his lips, I could see the hunger raging inside him. For an insane moment, I almost *wanted* him to give in to his urges and bite me. I shrank away from the thought immediately, hoping he wouldn't hear it and act on it. I wanted to feed him, to nourish him, but I didn't want to bleed, I didn't want to die…

Instead of puncturing me with his fangs, he climaxed inside me, and it was like a glacier, a shifting avalanche of cold ecstasy tumbling through me. I came hard, my back lifting off the bed in rapid spasms as I screamed his name over and over.

He hissed, his lips brushing against my throat for the barest instant…

… And then he withdrew sharply, standing up and buttoning his trousers with shaking fingers. There was a look in his eyes that was somewhere between starvation and regret. I tried to reach out to him with my mind again, but his thoughts clanged shut like iron gates, barring me from entry.

"Hey, what's wrong?" I asked, my voice trembling. "Are you okay?"

"Yes. I am fine. I must leave now. I have… other matters to attend to." It sounded like his accent was suddenly thicker somehow. "Please make yourself as comfortable as possible during my absence."

"Sure," I answered in a small voice.

He folded his wings tightly, pulled his tunic back on, and left abruptly.

I didn't need to read his mind to figure out that he was ashamed of what had just happened between us. Guess Valkred males aren't much different from human ones. They're all passion and flattery until about two seconds after they come, and then they can't wait to put as much distance as possible between themselves and the girls they've carelessly seduced. In his case, he's probably embarrassed that he slipped up for a moment and thought of a blood slave as a "mate." Now he's going to cover it up by acting like a heartless asshole.

Well, that was nothing new. I'd had plenty of horny shitheads flip that same switch on me, back on Earth.

Still, this time, it hurt more.

I supposed that based on the time I'd spent with Akzun, I'd managed to forget that he and Nos were the same species. I'd wanted to believe that the Valkred were better somehow, more advanced, more evolved than humans were.

I'd clearly been wrong about that. Fine.

So what now?

Would I stay in my bedchamber, staring at the walls and just waiting for him to decide to come back? When he did, would he drink my blood this time? Would he kill me just to shut the door on his own humiliation, to deny his feelings for me? To prove to Torqa and the other members of his race that he wasn't in my thrall, that I was just his property?

The creeping anxiety I'd felt when he first brought me to the palace was starting to return. Maybe I should go back to exploring the place and seeing if there might be some way to escape.

Maybe I'd succeed, and maybe I wouldn't.

But it was better than doing nothing.

I left the room, not bothering to skulk around this time. I figured I'd look a lot more suspicious to any guards who found me if I was creeping around in the shadows, but if I just walked normally with my head held high, they'd probably assume I'd accepted my fate was just displaying natural curiosity about my new surroundings.

I walked past Akzun's chamber and headed for the narrow, winding staircase made of vivid red marble. It was like walking down a waterfall of blood that had somehow been frozen in time. Sure enough, several armed guards passed me, barely glancing in my direction.

As I reached one of the lower levels, I heard a friendly voice call out from a nearby sitting room, "Taking some time to wander around a bit, are we?"

I turned and saw a tall, lanky Valkred leaning against the doorway with a smile on his face. He had long, curly purple hair that cascaded around his shoulders, and his green eyes glimmered with amusement.

"Not that I can blame you," he went on, stepping forward and extending his hand. "The Ruby Stronghold is full of fascinating artifacts and works of art, dating all the way back to the first Blood Ruler. It's a pleasure to formally meet you… Carly, is it?"

I shook his hand. "Yes. And you are…?"

"Zark."

The name was familiar to me, but it took me a few seconds to place it. "You're Akzun's brother, aren't you?"

"Indeed I am!" he replied, clapping his hands together happily. "I'm so pleased that you've heard of me. Now: Were you seeking out something specific? Perhaps I can help you… as long as it's not a way to escape, of course." His voice was cheerful, but there was something behind his eyes that made me think that he wasn't joking – that he knew *exactly* what I'd been looking for, and was doing his best to defuse the situation peacefully, rather than reporting me.

Well, that's nicer than he could have been.

"Actually, there is something you might be able to help me with," I began hesitantly. "Akzun left, and he didn't say when he'd be coming back. I don't know if you've, um, seen the bedroom he put me in…"

"I have," he said cannily, "and I believe I understand the problem. Your quarters are rather spartan, aren't they? Nothing much to do or see. You would like some games to occupy your mind? Some books, perhaps? Are you a reader?"

"I am, and yes, that would be lovely," I said. "Particularly the books. Since I'm new to your world, I'd welcome the chance to familiarize myself with your classic literature. It might help me gain a firmer understanding of your history, your culture…"

Zark laughed heartily. "My, but you're a sharp one! You're absolutely right – that's a splendid idea, and there are many engaging novels I can recommend to you for that very purpose, if you'd like to follow me to the leisure suite. It's located at the edge of the palace grounds. First, though, I'm afraid you'll have to accompany me on a brief and rather boring errand along the way."

"Certainly," I said, letting him lead me along a passageway that took us to the rear grounds of the palace. "What's the errand?"

"That," he replied, gesturing ahead of us.

It was still dark outside, but as my eyes adjusted, I could see an aerodynamic shape the size of a small house. There were numerous workers crawling all over it, using what looked like high-tech laser welding torches and other tools on its surface.

"I think I recognize that ship." I squinted at it, stepping a bit closer. "I've been on it before. It's Akzun's private shuttle, right?"

"Precisely," he nodded.

"And a fine shuttle it is." One of the workers stepped out from under the craft, wiping his pale hands on his overalls. He had sunken, bloodshot eyes and thin lips, but his demeanor seemed friendly enough. "Greetings. My name is Lun, and I'm the Blood Ruler's chief engineer."

"Nice to meet you," I said. "So, if it's such a fine shuttle, why are you guys tinkering with it?"

"Ah, well you may ask," Lun said with a grin that was more like a grimace. "When he used it to transport you to the planet's surface recently, Akzun noticed that it wasn't flying as smoothly as it's supposed to when he entered sub-orbital airspace. He ordered our ground crews to examine it. Sadly, though, our automated diagnostic programs don't appear to be functioning properly, forcing us to take a closer look."

"That's probably for the best. I've worked with auto-diagnostics before, and they can be finicky. When you come right down to it, the most reliable diagnostic software is right here." I pointed to my own eyes.

Lun seemed surprised. "Do you mean to tell me that you're familiar with advanced propulsion systems?"

"In a manner of speaking. I used to repair airplanes back on Earth. They're not built for off-world travel, of course, but when it comes to flying machines built to operate within a planet's atmosphere, a lot of the basic principles are the same. Mind if I take a closer look?"

He shrugged. "By all means. I'm sure I don't have to tell you the steep penalty for sabotaging a Valkred ship, especially the Blood Ruler's personal transport vessel?"

"Nah, I think I can guess."

I walked a slow circle around the shuttle, ignoring the startled looks from the Valkred who were working on it. Most of the alien tech was utterly beyond my comprehension – but there was one element that I definitely recognized and understood.

"It's the wings," I said quietly.

"What about them?" Lun inquired curiously. "They're largely decorative. Meant to represent the wings of the Valkred. To mimic their shape."

"Uh-huh, I'm sure they are," I replied. "And I'm betting that even with a functioning diagnostic program to plug this sucker into, your people would be focused on the engine drives, the stabilizers, the energy sources, and a hundred other pieces of hardware and software that are way over my head… all the stuff that's built in to get you from one planet or ship to another out in space, right?"

Lun nodded, silently encouraging me to continue.

"But once you're *within* a planetary atmosphere, the wings will affect how the craft moves," I continued. "They'll catch currents, updrafts, pressure changes. And if there are any flaws in the wings, even small ones, they might catch the air the wrong way and shake things up a bit. Maybe even pull you to one side or the other – or flip you upside down, if the flaws are deep enough. No, if I were you, I'd save myself a whole lot of time by checking to make sure you don't have any dents or dings going on there that are knocking you around during re-entry."

Lun climbed up the side of the shuttle with the grace and speed of a monkey scaling a tree, hopping over to one of the wings. He flung himself down on all fours, nosing around the wing as though he were literally trying to sniff out the problem. Finally, he called out triumphantly, standing up with a big smile.

"By the Succubi," he exclaimed, "you're right! There's a deep divot at the rear of the wing, near the bulkhead! That must be the source of the problem!"

He called down to the other workers in their native language and they sprang into action, eagerly crawling all over the wing like ants over a dropped piece of food.

Zark burst into applause. "Bravo, my dear! *Bravo!* A truly astounding display, to be sure! You're certainly proving more useful than most blood slaves. Now, if you'd like to browse our library?"

"Actually," I said, clearing my throat, "would it be okay if I stayed here for a while and watched them work on the shuttle? It's been so long since I've been around these kinds of machines, and I'd really love to take a closer look, maybe get my hands dirty."

Zark frowned. "You… want to make your hands unclean? I don't understand. I thought hygiene was important to Earthlings."

I giggled. "No, it's just an expression! It means I'd like to get involved, root around in the machinery, see what makes it work."

He looked to Lun, eyebrows raised. "Well, if Lun doesn't feel you'll be in his way…"

"Not at all!" Lun assured him. "I'd be fascinated to hear an off-worlder's perspective on our way of doing things. Who knows? She might even surprise us with more insights."

"Fair enough," Zark laughed. "Have fun, human! Get as dirty as you like! We'll have a laser-shower ready for you inside whenever you're done." He walked off, shaking his head in wonderment.

Lun turned to me. "So, tell me more about these flying machines you repaired! What sorts of weapons systems were they equipped with?"

Chapter Ten

Akzun

The moment after I'd climaxed with Carly, I was filled with a frustrated hunger that felt like it would drive me insane. Her neck, her blood, had been *so* close, flowing just beneath her flesh, begging to be drained…

But I couldn't.

I desperately wanted to, but I was too afraid of hurting her, or worse. I was terrified that once I started to drink from her, I wouldn't be able to stop myself until I'd consumed every last drop. And then what? I'd have lost her, wasted her utterly, just when I was starting to truly appreciate her companionship.

Still, my veins ached, and my mouth was as dry as the sand on the desert moon of Sha'Hara. My head was filled with a horrid buzzing, like a swarm of Gruulian venom-wasps stinging my brain to death.

I needed to do something. I needed to feed. Now.

As I made my hasty exit from Carly's bedchamber, I worried that she would find the manner of my sudden departure rude. I resolved to make it up to her as soon as I'd cleared my head and filled my stomach, but I couldn't focus on that now.

I walked to the platform over the sheer marble shaft and stepped off, allowing my wings to catch the air and gently carry me down to the bottom. Then I hurried to the lower levels of the Ruby Stronghold.

"The dungeons," I whispered to myself with a bitter laugh.

To be fair, that little falsehood had been a cruel joke to play on Carly when she first arrived. Certainly, the subterranean chambers had once fit that description, especially under the earlier Blood Rulers, who enjoyed keeping their blood slaves chained up in filthy cells and torturing them when they weren't feeding on them. Even the great, good-hearted reformer Kochak kept the slaves in harsh conditions during his rule. He didn't see the point in coddling them and dedicating resources to their comfort when they were simply a food source, nothing more.

No, *I* was the one who had decided that, although blood slaves were a necessary element of the Stronghold – a vital source of nutrition to all who lived and worked here – there was no reason to treat them poorly. I'd removed the chains and torture devices, cleansed the lower levels of mildew and vermin, converted the cells to small and spartan bedchambers, and insulated them to ensure that the occupants were kept at a comfortable temperature. The more well-behaved ones were even given a chance to borrow books and games from the leisure suite.

True, I'd continued to keep them on a diet of nutrient pastes – they *were* still prisoners, after all, kept here against their will because they were enemies of the Valkred in one way or another. And beyond just keeping them alive, the pastes added important vitamins to their blood and gave it a more robust flavor.

Still, I considered it to be progress. A sign that as a species, we were continuing to evolve and reject the more barbarous elements of our own past. Whoever the next Blood Ruler turned out to be – hopefully not for many, many more years – I fervently hoped that he or she would continue these practices.

Somehow, though, I doubted it.

I saw that there were a handful of servants who were in the process of feeding off the slaves. I met their gazes politely, waiting for them to finish. Sure enough, they nodded their understanding, concluded their meals quickly, and left me alone.

Some previous Blood Rulers had happily joined their servants in drinking from the slaves, but that had never seemed quite right to me. I didn't like to fraternize in such a way, to turn a basic survival need into an excuse for debauchery.

I preferred privacy while I fed.

I walked past the rows of chamber doors, contemplating my options. A handful of Krote pirates, a Drekkir pickpocket, a Xehrulian couple who'd been caught spying… none of them appealed to me at the moment. And naturally, Carly was the only human blood slave the palace had seen for years.

Ah. A Mana. One who'd been taken prisoner after a particularly gruesome battle near Nanryr.

Not perfect. But he'd have to do.

I approached the open door of his chamber, peering into the darkness. He looked back at me with his fishy eyes, too pale and weak to stand, his expression unreadable. As I stared at him, it was difficult not to be reminded of M'ruvev – and suddenly, I was filled with a horrible rage.

Damn M'ruvev.

Damn him for being under attack by Krote corsairs when my ship happened to be passing by, so I'd end up making "friends" with a sworn enemy. Damn him for insisting that we meet at The Vein, for exploiting my weaknesses when he owed me his life. Damn him for whatever foul technology or sorcery he'd used to make his flagship disappear before my eyes, for forcing me to agree to a list of terms that clearly benefited his race far more than mine. Damn him for giving me five days to find out who assaulted his ship, for putting me in an impossible position, for making my own people turn on me, for making me suffer through my hunger, damn him, *damn him!*

I saw the flicker of fear in the Mana slave's eyes just before I closed the distance between us, a blur in the darkness, a flash of fangs in the gloom as I sank my teeth into his wrist. He knew not to bother fighting back – he'd been drank from far too many times already for that – but still, something inside him clearly understood that there was anger behind my bite this time. I heard his heart rate quicken, and I even got a brief flash of his thoughts in my mind:

Is *this* it? Is this the last bite, the one that will finally kill me?

His blood spurted against my tongue, brackish and briny, and I gorged myself on it greedily. I wanted to drink from his throat – as many of my servants had before, based on the previous bite marks – but I couldn't trust myself to do so without finishing him off, which would be a needless loss of life, not to mention wasteful.

I swallowed. And swallowed. And swallowed.

I felt the oxygen carried in the Mana's blue blood cells flowing through my own veins, giving me strength, power – control over myself again. The buzzing in my head faded, replaced with a magnificent silence that allowed me to hear my own thoughts once more.

"Nnnh," the Mana grunted quietly, closing his eyes and leaning his head back with a soft shudder.

My attention returned sharply to what I was doing. Had I gone too far? Was he close to death? I felt like I had lost all control, and it shook me more than I wanted to admit.

With great effort, I pulled my fangs out of his wrist, withdrawing from him.

As I retreated to the door, the Mana opened his eyes again, heaving a sigh. "I wish you'd finished it this time," he gurgled faintly.

I raised an eyebrow. "You would prefer death, then, to your life here?"

He gave a feeble nod. "By the stars, yes. Anything… would be better than… this." And with that, he fell over onto his cot, passing out.

I slammed the door to his chamber and stalked back through the lower level corridors, feeling fresh anger surge inside me. All of my reforms, all of my attempts to show respect to these prisoners, all the criticism I'd endured for "treating them like guests instead of slaves" – and they wished for *death* instead?

Such a lack of gratitude!

"Many of your predecessors felt the same rage toward the blood slaves in their charge," Torqa's voice interjected behind me. "Would you like me to show you how they chose to express such hostilities? I believe we still have some of the old implements of torture around here somewhere. We can use them on the prisoners together, if you wish. It would be… fun."

I turned to her, curling my lip furiously. "No. Thank you."

She barked a humorless laugh, leaning against the stone wall. "I thought not. I must admit, I'm surprised to find you down here drinking from the same dirty wrists and necks that your servants have been sucking on, instead of upstairs feeding from your untouched blood slave."

"The way you spoke to her earlier was wholly unnecessary," I said through gritted teeth, "and will not be tolerated again."

"Really? How odd. I've said far worse to the other blood slaves in this castle without drawing your ire. Unless, of course, it is as I suspected," she went on: "You don't consider her to be just a blood slave, do you? No, despite the number of noble Valkred women who would be eager to share your bed and your life, you prefer to think of that squealing pink creature upstairs as a potential mate. How disgusting, not to mention disappointing."

"Your disappointment matters little to me, Torqa. And whether I consider her a mate or not is none of your business. You will obey me in this matter."

Torqa gave me an exaggerated bow once more. "Very well, Blood Ruler. Your word is law, as ever. I only came down here to let you know that M'ruvev has been attempting to contact you."

"Oh? Why?"

"He wanted you to know that he's doing his best to honor the deadline he gave you, but that he's been facing a lot of pressure from his own people. He's not entirely confident that he can keep them at bay for much longer." She took a deep breath, then added, "He also said that his people managed to recover some wreckage from one of the Valkred ships that the Aquavor fired upon before it was destroyed. They weren't able to gather much organic matter, but the fragments they did retrieve appear to contain Valkred DNA."

"So it was our own people who broke the treaty."

"It seems that way, yes," she answered. "They've sent the data to us. I'm cross-referencing it against the organic materials we keep archived for our warriors. Hopefully, a match will turn up soon."

"Good. Keep me informed."

"I will. Oh, and Akzun?"

I waited for her to continue, annoyed.

Torqa smiled nastily. "It may interest you to know that your 'mate' is currently on your private docking pad with Lun and his work crew. Not that it's *any of my business*, of course, as you said."

"What the blazes is she doing there?" I roared, a spike of jealousy driving through me.

Torqa's smirk melted into a grin and made her resemble a Truvilian Gore-Shark. "Why don't you go and see for yourself, O' Wise and Noble Leader?"

I marched to the docking area, seething. Damn it, didn't everyone in this infernal palace know that Carly was mine alone? And now I find out she's fraternizing with my servants?

Just another ungrateful blood slave, throwing my kindness back in my face, cursing the hospitality I offer. Well, we'll see about that.

The door to the castle grounds opened before me and I stepped through briskly, hearing laughter echo across the tarmac. Sure enough, there was Carly, sitting on the wing of my private shuttle surrounded by Lun and his workers.

"So you mean to tell me," Lun cackled, "that on your world, the Earthlings take a great sense of accomplishment in squeezing into the tiny waste disposal chambers on these… these *air-planes* you speak of, and *mating* in them mid-flight?"

"Yep!" Carly replied cheerfully. "They call it joining the Mile-High Club."

"*Mile*-high," one of the other workers scoffed. "As though that's something to be proud of, ha! Well, I suppose if most of them ever get a chance to ride on a ship that leaves orbit, we know the first thing they'll probably try to do."

"*Join the Seventy-Mile-High Club!*" Carly and the others giggled in unison.

I couldn't believe my ears. "What the hell is going on here?" I demanded.

Everyone immediately fell silent.

Chapter Eleven

Carly

I turned to look at Akzun, surprised by the anger in his voice. What could I possibly have done wrong? He'd made such a point of not treating me like a slave or a prisoner. Wouldn't he *want* me to make myself comfortable, to make friends with the people here, to try to settle in and have fun?

"Hi Akzun," I chirped, trying to sound as casual as possible. "Is everything okay? You seem a little –"

"Get down from there," he interrupted coldly. "Now."

I glanced at Lun, and saw that his bloodshot eyes were full of fear. "We should go," he murmured to the other workers quietly, scuttling down the side of the shuttle. The others quickly followed suit, clearing the area.

"My apologies, Blood Ruler," Lun said as he passed Akzun, giving him a wide berth. "We meant no offense, I assure you. We were only –"

"You were only having unauthorized and inappropriate contact with my personal blood slave, and telling ribald jokes in her presence," Akzun snarled. "I will deal with you later, Lun."

Lun nodded, vanishing into the shadows and leaving me alone with Akzun. I slid down the bulkhead of the shuttle, landing easily on my feet and walking over to him.

"Why would you talk to Lun and the others like that?" I asked, the early embers of anger lighting up my belly. "They seem like nice guys."

"Then perhaps you'd prefer to take up residence in the lower levels with the other blood slaves after all," he countered fiercely, "so you can spend as much time with them as you please, and let *them* mate with you and drink from you without my interference."

I stomped over to him, furious now. "Okay, just what the hell is your problem here? First you have sex with me while putting thoughts in my head about how I'm your *mate*, then afterward you leave so fast you practically fly out the window – and now you're getting in my face about making harmless conversation with the people who work here. Would you mind telling me what's going on? Because personally, I'm starting to think you're just confused and angry at yourself for not being able to decide if you want to drink me, fuck me, or marry me, and you're taking it out on me!"

"It didn't sound like 'harmless conversation' to me," Akzun snapped. "It sounded like you were flirting."

"Well, I wasn't. I was being friendly, and trying to find out more about your people and their ways so I could communicate with you on a deeper level. But if you're going to fly into some stupid jealous rage every time I talk to someone who's not you, I'm not sure I even want to."

"This is not the place for us to have this discussion," Akzun growled, grabbing me and unfurling his wings.

I struggled, but I knew he was stronger than I was. Still, I refused to give him the satisfaction of seeing me just give in and let him take me wherever he wanted. "Put me down!"

"No. If you're going to live here with me, you need to learn the proper decorum. And if you don't want to live with me, then I suppose I'd better prepare accommodations for you in the dungeons." He picked me up and took off, flying us toward the highest tower of the palace.

I almost screamed for him to let go of me, then realized it would be a poor choice of words, given the circumstances. Instead, I maintained a stony silence all the way to the tower, then shoved him away as soon as we were inside his chamber.

"I'm sick of all this confusion and uncertainty," I told him hotly. "One minute it seems like you're trying to wine and dine me, and the next, you're pushing me around like you fucking own me. You want to treat me like I'm just a slave? Fine. Go ahead. I was a slave at Nos's place, and I can be one here, too. Lock me up, drink my blood, whatever. You want me to be your *mate* or your *consort* or whatever medieval bullshit you want to call a romantic relationship? Cool, okay, we can certainly give that a shot. But either way, act like a true Blood Ruler and *make a real decision*."

I turned and ran out into the hall, entering my own bedchamber and slamming the door behind me. My impulse was to lock it – but then I remembered the original purpose of this room, and that it locked from the outside, not the inside. So I pushed the bed against the door, blocking it just as Akzun started to pound on it.

"How *dare* you talk to me about what it means to be a Blood Ruler?" he yelled. "You don't have any idea of how things work here, or the responsibilities I carry!"

"Yeah, and from what I've seen, I don't *want* to!" I shouted back, tears stinging my eyes. "You brood and make grand speeches and wallow in self-pity, but when it comes down to it, you're too chicken-shit to even admit to yourself how you really feel about me and fucking act on it!"

"Open this door, Carly. Damn you! You know I can come in any time I choose!"

"Hey, you want to break the door down so you can scream at me some more face to face? Knock yourself out, asshole!"

"Do you even *want* to be my mate?" he challenged. "Or do you really want to live with the blood slaves below, and be food for my servants?"

"*I want to go home!*" I shrieked. Now I *was* crying. I couldn't believe it. Just a short while ago, I'd been brought here under duress, and now I found myself caring enough about Akzun that his cruel behavior actually hurt my feelings. Christ, what a strange turn of events.

"This *is* your home now, human!" Akzun roared. "Perhaps you'd better sit alone for a while and think on that before we speak again."

I heard him stalk down the hall to his own room and slam the door.

I threw myself down on the bed angrily, wiping my tears on the pillows. No matter what planet you're on, Carly, the men are all the same: Instead of confronting their emotions and dealing with them, they yell and posture and stomp around. *He's* the psychic, but he treats me like *I'm* the one who's the goddamn mind reader. Terrific. Now what do I do?

My thoughts drifted to the private shuttle parked right outside the castle. Lun had shown me so many of its systems and features. He'd babbled a lot of technical jargon at me glibly, thinking it would all be completely over my head.

But it wasn't. Not all of it, anyhow.

I still didn't fully understand the energy that allowed the ship to break the speed of light, but I did have some understanding of how that energy was channeled, and the controls used to pilot the shuttle. Manually, of course – the star charts programmed into the ship for navigation were utterly beyond me, since I was totally unfamiliar with this part of the galaxy.

Could I make the thing take off, if I put my mind to it? Probably. Could I figure out how to operate the basic programs, like life support and artificial gravity? I was reasonably certain that I could, yes.

Could I bring the weapons online, aim them, and fire them, if it came to that?

Yeah. I thought so.

And the hell of it was, during the time I spent with Lun, I hadn't seen any guards patrolling the perimeter of the tarmac. It was within the palace walls, after all, so Akzun's security staff probably thought no one would be able to get close enough to it to warrant posting guards around it.

The more I thought about it, the less escape seemed like an abstract concept instead of a real possibility. I wouldn't have to make my way to the exterior of the castle – just from the tower to the docking pad.

Carly, this is the most harebrained scheme ever conceived outside of an "I Love Lucy" episode, and you damn well know it, my brain lectured me sternly. *Let's say you can somehow evade an entire palace full of guards and get down to the docking pad. Okay. Let's say your confidence in your ability to fly a fucking alien spaceship is based on reality instead of idiotic delusions of grandeur. Fine. You honestly think no one would come after you? This whole planet's at war with those fish people... you think there aren't any planetary defense networks that would swat you out of the sky immediately? Hell, for all you know, they can remote-control the ship and shut it down. Or blow it up. Oh, and assuming you manage to get past all that through sheer dumb luck, what then? You said it yourself: You have no idea where you are in relation to Earth, and the star charts are useless gibberish. What are you going to do? Just pick a direction to fly in, and hope you get it right? Odds are, you'll run into some other hostile species. One that wants to dissect you and probe your insides. Or lay eggs in your chest, or something equally horrible.*

I shivered. I knew my chances of escape were slim to none. But more than that: Despite Akzun's behavior, there was some part of me that didn't *want* to leave him. The sex we'd had – the way our minds and hearts were connected, the way his body felt against mine, his passion for me – it was like nothing I'd ever experienced on Earth.

I wanted more of it.

God help me, I wanted him to stop yelling at me and start kissing me again.

Yeah, that's real romantic stuff. But what if he's done smooching and caressing me? What if he really does decide to toss me down in the basement, for the other people in the castle to suck my blood whenever they get peckish? What then, huh?

I didn't know. I felt like I didn't know anything anymore.

I curled up on the blanket, letting the tears come. I felt like I was losing my mind, like my heart was being torn in half.

I couldn't take much more of this.

Chapter Twelve

Akzun

I paced around my chamber like a Krowbian Flame-Tiger, raging inwardly at Carly, at Lun, at Torqa and M'ruvev – but most of all, at myself.

"Having some trouble keeping the human woman in line?"

I turned and found Zark sitting on the sill of the open window, a smile on his face.

"Something like that." I sighed. "I paid a fortune for her, Zark, and now that I have her, I must confess: I have no idea what to do with her."

"That's not terribly surprising." Zark hopped down from the window. "I know you haven't spent a tremendous amount of time around human females – you've only had brief encounters with them during your diplomatic visits to Earth, to consult with their rulers. But they're far more mercurial than Valkred women. Carly simply needs time to adjust. The only question is, will your temper allow you to grant her that time? Or would you rather assign her a cell in the lower levels and be done with it? If so, please let me know so I can be first in line to have a drink."

The jealousy flared within me again, but one look in Zark's eyes told me that he wasn't being serious – he was just teasing me, trying to get a rise out of me.

Brothers. They always know just which buttons to push, don't they?

"I can't do that," I said reluctantly.

"Then you should probably stop threatening her with it, don't you think?" Zark turned a chair backward and straddled it, resting his arms on its back. It was an affectation that had always bothered me, and he knew it – he was still trying to provoke me. "After all, empty threats are not the tools of a wise or effective ruler."

"So you've come to tell me what it means to be a good ruler, as well?" I snapped. "Wonderful. You're the third one today. Perhaps I should call in the cook or one of the cleaning staff, and get *their* opinions about the best way to lead an empire, too."

"Now you're just being silly, brother. Have you told her that you want her to be your mate?"

"Not exactly. I… may have let it slip telepathically, while we were…" I trailed off.

He winced, drawing air through his teeth in a pained hiss. "That is *so* much worse. Her species doesn't have psychic abilities – well, most of them don't, anyway. She doesn't understand that even if what we communicate nonverbally is what we might truly mean, our feelings must be ratified to each other out loud, to cement it. Otherwise, how is she supposed to know what's real and what's just a fleeting desire or fantasy? Especially when you don't even seem sure of which it is yourself."

"It's this thrice-damned *bloodlust!*" I said, exasperated. "Even now that I've consumed blood from one of the slaves in the dungeons, I still can't shake its effects! I still can't tell the difference between my senseless cravings and what I truly want for myself. It's ripping me apart! How am I supposed to rule my people – to end this war – if I can't even make sense of my own actions?"

Zark shrugged, not unkindly. "When it comes to what you should do about Carly, or how to separate your bloodlust from your real feelings, I'm afraid I have no idea what to tell you. Except that if you give her a chance, she might be the one who's able to save you from yourself. Which you would dismiss as nothing more than nonsensical romantic idealism, no doubt."

"I probably would."

"I suspected as much. *But,*" Zark went on cheerfully, "when it comes to leading your people and ending the war, well, that's something I might be in a better position to help you with."

"Oh?" I raised an eyebrow. "How so?"

"Torqa found a match for the DNA M'ruvev sent us in our military index. A warrior in the Fifth Fleet named Gruk."

"So this Gruk was the one who helped steal our ships and used them to attack the Aquavor?"

Zark shook his head. "Not quite. The DNA matched *partially*, but not exactly. Gruk only has one living relative: a cousin named Marug. One who's spoken out publicly against the treaty with the Mana. We tracked him down and got a precise match from the organic matter on the debris. His alibi didn't hold up. He was the one piloting the Valkred ship that got damaged during the assault."

"If he wasn't a real warrior, no wonder the Mana managed to tag him with their blasters a couple of times," I mused. "But who were the other pilots in the attack? For that matter, how did he gain access to our military craft for unauthorized use? All of the vessels in our fleet are heavily guarded."

"I don't know about you," Zark said, "but I'm inclined to believe that he had help from someone on the inside, and Torqa agrees with me. Marug is being subjected to her tender mercies at the Detention Facility even as we speak."

"Then we'd better join her at once," I replied.

"I knew you'd think so. After all, we wouldn't want her to have all the fun, would we?"

Moments later, Zark and I were riding toward the Detention Center in my personal armored hover-car. Palace guards on hover-cycles rode ahead and behind, keeping an eye out for potential threats.

Threats. The faces and buildings of the capitol city flew past me in a blur, and I couldn't help but think of my recent outing with Carly – or, more specifically, its rather tragic conclusion. Would exposing these renegades and ending the war with the Mana be enough to make my public look at me differently, to finally accept and celebrate me as their Blood Ruler? Or would they always find my leadership insufficient, especially if I did make Carly my mate? Would they merely be waiting for their next excuse to throw objects at us and call us names?

I wish I knew. Instead, all I could do was try to focus on the task at hand. Which certainly wasn't easy.

When we arrived at the Detention Center, armed officers met us at the gates, leading us into the innermost cells – the ones reserved for the most dangerous enemies of the state, the ones where prisoners were subjected to hideously inventive torments until they gave up their secrets.

The ones designed by Torqa herself.

"You'll want to put these on, sir," one of the guards said, handing a pair of helmets to me and Zark. They were outfitted with thick, tinted visors. We were given heavy sets of gloves as well.

"What are these for?" Zark asked, putting them on.

The guard winced. "You'll see."

The cell door slid open, and we stepped inside.

It felt like we had stepped onto the surface of a sun as it was about to go nova. I squinted, recoiling against the intense heat.

"I believe you've taken us to the wrong room," Zark said to the guard. "This appears to be the sauna."

Every inch of the walls, ceilings, and floors was glowing with intense purplish-white ultraviolet rays. A young Valkred was suspended in the middle of the room, naked, hanging from a series of tubes and wires like a defenseless insect caught in the strands of a predator's web.

His skin burned bright red, and it took me a few moments to realize that entire sections of his flesh had been stripped of multiple layers – in some areas, I could even see through it to the organs and sinews beneath. He was pitifully skeletal, his skin stretched tightly over his skull and bones. The surface membranes of his eyeballs were dried out, making it impossible for him to even blink. Most of his hair had fallen out, and lay on the floor around him in clumps, smoldering against the heat lamps and filling the air with its burning stink.

And he was screaming. By the stars, he was screaming louder than any creature I'd ever heard before.

"Ah, gentlemen! Welcome!" Torqa raised her voice to be heard over the din. She raised a glass of artificial blood in our direction. "Would either of you care for a drink?"

"No, thank you," I said, examining the apparatus that was holding the prisoner in place. "This is the offender, I assume?"

"Indeed. This is Marug, who allowed his hatred of the Mana to overwhelm his loyalty to his own people. Who chose to steal a fighter craft and take it on a joy ride that ended with the senseless destruction of the Aquavor. I hope you'll forgive him for not bowing before you, Blood Ruler, given the circumstances."

"Dare I ask about the particulars of his current accommodations?" Zark asked. He was trying to sound upbeat, but I could hear how queasy the sight made him. He knew the importance of securing the empire and severely punishing those who threatened its interests, but he had no stomach for torture.

Torqa's incessant sneering and posturing may be almost unbearable, but at times like these, I'm reminded of just how valuable she can be.

"I'm delighted that you asked!" Torqa said eagerly. "As you can see, the removal of the epidermis allows the ultraviolet rays to essentially cook the little traitor from the inside out, even as these tubes feed a very special concoction into his veins – a chemical compound of my own invention, which robs the nutrients from his body at a vastly accelerated rate. He's starving for blood." She leaned in close to the prisoner, teasing him. "But we won't let you die of thirst, will we? No, it will only feel that way, a dozen times over, until you *tell us what we need to know*."

"*I can't!*" Marug eyed the glass of red fluid just out of his reach, his tongue scraping like sandpaper against his lips. I could tell that he wanted to weep, but his tear ducts were so dry and irritated they looked like cured meat. "You *know* I can't! You *know* what will happen to me! Please, *please*, just kill me and be done with it!"

"There's no need for that," I said, stepping closer and trying to hide my revulsion at the sight of him. Large patches of salt were dried on his torso, flaking off and hitting the floor every time he tried to wriggle against his bonds. "We don't want to kill you, Marug. We don't even truly want to torture you."

"Speak for yourself," Torqa said with a laugh. "I'm having a lovely time! Why, I'm hoping you continue to resist – I could happily do this all night!"

I ignored her words, doing my best to keep my focus on Marug. "You are an idealist, committed to your beliefs. I understand that. In a way, I even find it commendable. You saw what you perceived to be injustice, and you took bold action to correct it. But you've been caught, and now you must face the consequences. If you simply tell us who you were working with, and who granted you access to military vessels…"

"*I told you, I can't!*" he wailed, his terrified eyes flickering over to Torqa. No doubt he was dreading another round of anguish from her. I couldn't blame him one bit.

I took a breath and tried again. "If you cooperate with us, your pain will end, and you will be granted a life sentence instead of execution. Now please, be reasonable. Don't force us to continue this horror."

He hung his head, shook it gently, and mumbled something under his breath.

"What was that?" I leaned in even more closely, straining to hear. "What did you say?"

Marug raised his head again, staring directly into my eyes. His skin was burning so vividly I could feel the heat coming off him in waves, smell his innards roasting.

"I said you don't understand," he whimpered. "But you will. Soon."

Suddenly, Marug's arm snapped free of the bonds that were holding it in place. I tried to leap back, away from him, but I was too slow.

He snatched my sidearm from its holster on my hip, pressed the barrel to his temple, and pulled the trigger.

His brains hit the floor in a gruesome spatter, sizzling against the ultraviolet panels.

He slumped in the restraints, dead.

"*Damn it!*" Torqa shrieked, storming over to the door. It slid open, and she yelled into the corridor: "*I swear to all the Succubi, whoever secured this prisoner's restraints is going to answer to me!*"

I stared at Marug's remains, dumbfounded.

M'ruvev's deadline was fast approaching – and the one solid lead we'd had just evaporated before my eyes. We still had no idea how to find the other members involved in this conspiracy, or how to stop them from stealing more ships and waging their own private war against the Mana.

We were back to square one, with nothing to show for it.

Chapter Thirteen

Carly

I sat on my bed, operating a small data pad that Dhako had delivered to me. His English wasn't very good, but based on what he said, I was fairly certain that Zark had asked him to bring it to me.

The inscription on the main screen appeared to confirm that: *"Carly- This will give you access to the books in the leisure suite's library. For your entertainment and edification, may I recommend that you start with File 17Ø2911Q? -Z"*

That was… shockingly nice of him. His brother could learn some manners from him, that's for sure.

Still, I had to admit that even though Zark seemed friendly and charming, Akzun was the one I couldn't banish from my thoughts.

It took me a few minutes, but I managed to figure out how to make the data pad work. Zark had been kind enough to reprogram the language option to English, so I didn't have to fumble and guess at it too much. I took his advice and chose the file he'd suggested.

When I started to get a sense of what I was reading, I couldn't help but laugh. It appeared to be a novel written over a century ago, a story about a Blood Ruler who, improbably and against the advice of the palace advisors, chose a human mate. The genders were swapped, but the similarity to my own situation was still kind of eerie.

I flipped through the scanned pages, eager to find out what would happen to these star-crossed lovers. In the story, the Valkred practically revolted when they learned that their leader had chosen a human consort instead of a member of her own race. It destabilized the Valkred empire's standing in the galaxy, inviting other species to take advantage of the dissension and attempt conquest. It drove a wedge between the Blood Ruler and the members of her family. It caused tremendous drama and utter chaos. Their union appeared to be completely doomed.

But…

As I reached the final chapters, I found that – just like in most Earth stories – the seemingly insurmountable conflicts between the main characters were still resolved with a happy ending. The human male managed to prove himself a worthy mate, and against all odds, became a hero to the people of Valkred. The palace staff, the Blood Ruler's family… everyone accepted him in the end, and the two were wed.

"And they lived happily ever after." I chuckled wryly. I guess some things are just universal.

Had Zark given me this book to give me hope? To show me that the idea of a Valkred Blood Ruler choosing a human mate wasn't entirely unheard of here, even if it had just been relegated to fiction so far? To make me believe that it might be possible for me to have a future with Akzun after all, if I could only find some way to distinguish myself to him and to the rest of the Valkred?

It was a nice thought.

Then I thought about Torqa, and a shudder of pure revulsion went through me. Try as I might, I couldn't quite conceive of anything I could do to ever get *her* on my side. Especially since I was relatively sure that most of her ire toward me sprung from the fact that she wanted Akzun all to herself. It wasn't anything she'd said, exactly – but as a woman, it was an undeniable dynamic that I'd recognized plenty of times on Earth. As long as I stood between her and the man of her dreams, I'd be her enemy.

And as enemies went, she seemed like a damn dangerous one.

I heard movement outside my door, and my heart skipped a beat. All these thoughts of Torqa were making me skittish. It was probably just Akzun, returning to his chambers. Fine. He could do whatever the hell he wanted. I was in no mood to talk to him after the scene he'd made earlier.

He should take some time to cool off. He could certainly use it. Besides, now that I've got this data pad, I've got plenty of books to read in order to pass the time…

Then I heard something crash across the hall.

So what? He's throwing a tantrum and breaking things in his room. That seems about his speed. Best to leave him to it. Ugh, men, I swear to God. Impossible to deal with in any galaxy.

… but it didn't sound like someone was tearing up the room. There was a long silence, then another thump and crash.

Then silence again.

I was starting to feel uneasy. What was going on over there?

I hopped off my bed, moved it away from the door, and poked my head out. The corridor was empty. The door to Akzun's chamber was ajar.

And beyond that… darkness.

I stepped out apprehensively, squinting my eyes at Akzun's room, trying to see what, if anything, was inside. It didn't look like there was any movement. I didn't hear any sounds or breathing.

Somehow, though, I felt like there was a presence inside, watching me. I didn't know how. I could just *sense* it.

A chill went up my spine, and for a moment, I was a little kid again, cringing and cowering in the shadows of my room after my parents had gone to sleep, feeling the darkness press in on me from all sides. Imagining a hundred nightmarish shapes crawling and slithering and panting in the corners, teeth bared, waiting for me to fall asleep so they could devour me.

I had begged my mom and dad for a night light many times, but they refused. Instead, they just kept patting me on the head and insisting that the more nights I spent in the dark, the sooner I'd realize there was nothing to be afraid of. Later, when I got older, I came to understand that they were too poor to afford anything as extravagant as a night light, or the additional energy costs of keeping it plugged in.

Meanwhile, though, my fear of the dark never fully left me, even as an adult.

And now the dark doorway was gaping in front of me, mocking me, like a portal to madness and oblivion. I wanted to throw my terror aside, charge into the room, and prove to myself that there was no reason to be afraid.

But I couldn't, not any more than I could have when I was a child.

"Akzun?" I called out, my voice trembling. "Are you in there?"

Nothing. Just shadows and silence.

Except something inside me – something horrible and undeniable – insisted that there *was* someone there. That eyes were staring at me, waiting for me to turn my back so something could lunge and pounce and bite and tear. The same boogeyman from my childhood, one with a thousand faces, one that had followed me across entire star systems to satisfy his hunger.

Oh, stop being so goddamn ridiculous, Carly! I chided myself. *You get abducted by a flying saucer, enslaved by a space vampire, bought by another,* threatened *by a third, and* this *is what you're afraid of? An empty fucking room? Grow up! There are very real dangers and monsters all around you, so maybe focus on those instead of imaginary ones, okay?*

I took a deep breath.

Okay.

I took a few steps backward – still waiting for something wild and ugly and awful to spring out of the darkness – then steeled myself and turned around, heading for the marble stairway. I went down one level, then another. My stomach was rumbling, and I wondered if I might be able to find a kitchen or pantry of some kind.

Sure enough, I eventually found a chamber where every surface seemed to be either polished steel or patterns of black and red ceramic. It was hard to tell, but the fixtures and machines bolted to the walls and counters looked like they might have been cooking appliances. I opened a few cabinets with heavy metal doors – the inside of one of them felt refrigerated, and about a dozen bags of red fluid were hanging inside.

Probably more of that "artificial blood" gunk - I'm definitely not drinking that.

"Do you require assistance?" a raspy voice behind me asked.

I turned and saw Dhako. He stood at attention in the doorway, his eyebrows raised expectantly.

"Um, yes, thank you," I answered. "I was hoping I could find something to eat?"

"Of course. Please follow me."

Dhako brought me to a dining room with a long table, gesturing for me to sit. "I will return momentarily with your food," he said. "Until then, please make yourself as comfortable as possible."

Just as I was about to take a seat, my eye was drawn to a tall window overlooking a fascinating garden. I wasn't sure why, but I felt it calling to me – perhaps because sitting outside and admiring the natural beauty of my surroundings would make me feel less like Akzun's prisoner and more like his guest.

"I don't mean to be difficult," I called out after Dhako, "but would it be possible for me to eat out there?"

He nodded placidly. "Certainly. Have a seat in the garden, and I'll bring your meal to you directly."

"Thanks."

I found my way down to the garden and sat at a small, round metal table with a glass top, taking in my surroundings. A string of delicate yellow lights were draped all around me, held up by tall stakes that blended wonderfully with the trees.

The flora and fauna of Valkred were beautiful and intriguing – I couldn't take my eyes off the gnarled black bushes with their metallic leaves of purple and blue, or the bizarre insect species crawling and fluttering around the lush petals of the alien flowers. There were vividly-hued caterpillars almost twelve inches long; pale moths, with long curled tails and intricate patterns on their wings; bees that were half the size of my palm, humming sleepy lullabies to themselves, their furry bodies speckled with a variety of dried, fragrant nectars that glowed in the dark.

So many sights to take in! So many new species to learn about and appreciate! How could I possibly still want to go back to my dull, hardscrabble life on Earth, when there were so many breathtaking sights and sounds to take in here on Valkred?

Just as that thought crossed my mind, the lights blinked out, darkness rapidly swooping in to cover my eyes tightly and claim me for its own.

My breath caught in my throat. I held my hands a few inches in front of my face, moving my fingers, but I couldn't see a thing. It was as though I'd been suddenly struck blind, flailing and helpless, waiting for the predators of the night to carry me away forever.

"Hello?" I called out tremulously. "Is anyone there? What's going on?"

I heard something flapping in the sky over me, and felt a shape closing in on me swiftly from directly above. I threw my hands over my head and cried out, twisting out of my chair sharply and throwing myself on the grass to avoid whatever was coming down on me. On the way down, I twisted my ankle, feeling it give out under me.

There was a loud smashing sound on the ground right next to me, and something sharp and jagged dug into my arm. I shrieked, horribly certain that I'd been right, that some winged, razor-mouthed beast had sunk its teeth in me and was about to chew the flesh off my bones. I swung my fists in its direction, desperately trying to fight it off. I expected to connect with a furry snout and cruel tusks, to feel its hot breath on my hand, to hear the thing growl and grunt and slobber.

Then the lights flickered back on, illuminating the ground around me.

The first thing I saw was my own blood, smeared across my sleeve and dripping on the pearly blades of grass. I looked around for whatever had attacked me, but all I could see was the shattered remains of what appeared to be a stone statue. I could still vaguely make out the crouched legs, and part of a bat wing. The rest was mostly rubble – and from the look of it, the sharp, broken edges were what had gouged my arm. A sliver of its hideous face stared up at me, fangs bared.

I peered up at the towers of the palace, and saw where the statue had fallen from. It was one of a row of sculpted figures perched on the battlements, depicting fierce snarling creatures with long claws. They reminded me of the gargoyles that guarded the walls of the few remaining gothic cathedrals on Earth, set there to frighten evil spirits away.

I dragged myself to my feet and started limping toward the doorway that led back inside the castle. Between the freaky power outage and the falling objects, I decided that dining *al fresco* that night might not be such a good idea after all. My arm hurt, and pain stabbed at my ankle, but I still managed to make it most of the way before a shadow fell across me.

It was Akzun, staring at me with his piercing dark eyes, his expression intense but unreadable.

Chapter Fourteen

Akzun

When I saw the blood pouring out of Carly's arm, my pulse quickened immediately, beads of sweat forming all across my flesh. The smell of her blood was so heavy that it went straight to my head. It was all I could do not to drop to my hands and knees and lick it off the grass – or worse, seize her arm and start gulping it straight from the wound.

Instead, I did everything I could to keep my face and posture as neutral as possible. I didn't want her to know how deeply thirsty she was making me, how much I wanted to devour her in a series of long, warm, wonderful drafts.

"What has happened here?" I asked, keeping my jaw tightly clenched in an attempt to control my cravings.

"Oh, hey, welcome home," she replied with a weak laugh. "Yeah, I, uh, must look like a real mess, huh? First I went looking for some food, then I asked Dhako if I could sit outside while I ate and he said yes, and then the next thing I knew the lights went out and one of those statues up on the tower came loose and almost killed me… I got a little scraped up, and I think I twisted my ankle, but I'm sure I'll be okay."

My nostrils were filled with the rusty scent of blood. My brain felt like someone was running an electric current through it. I couldn't stand it anymore. I needed a place to focus my aggression, a valve to release the pressure building relentlessly in my skull. I needed to take my bloodlust out on someone, anyone.

Dhako appeared in the doorway behind me, fretting and wringing his hands. "Oh dear! Is she all right?"

I whirled on him, roaring. "*I leave her in your care, and* this *is what I come home to? You were supposed to be looking after her, damn you!*"

Dhako took a step backward, his eyes wide. "I… I offer my deepest and most sincere apologies, Blood Ruler. You are correct, of course, I should not have left her unattended…"

"Hey, no, don't yell at him for this!" Carly piped up, putting a hand on my shoulder. "It wasn't his fault! He was just getting the food for me, it's not like he could watch me every single second. It was just an accident, it could have happened to anyone!"

By the stars, the *blood!* I had to get her to the healer as quickly as possible so the wound could be closed, before I completely lost control of myself.

"I'll deal with you later, Dhako – but for now, send Khim up to the tower at once," I snarled, turning to Carly. "Come, let's get you up to your chamber and wait for the healer to tend to you."

Dhako nodded, running off.

"I'm sure that's not necessary," Carly protested. "All I need is a bandage for the scrapes on my arm and some time for my ankle to straighten out again. I'll be just fine."

I shook my head insistently. "No, we must be sure you're not more gravely injured. Now take hold of me, and I'll fly you up to your room."

"Well, I *do* like it when you flap me around from place to place." She gave me a bashful smile. "Okay, you win. Let's go."

I lifted her up quickly before she could change her mind, flexed my wings to their fullest span, and took off for the tower window. Her blood was soaking into my tunic, and my desire felt like hot wires being inserted in my brain, deeper and deeper.

"Wow, the view's so much cooler when I'm not looking at it from behind a window!" she breathed in my ear.

"I'm glad you enjoy it. I shall have to, as you say, *flap* you around the palace grounds more often."

Carly laughed. "I'd like that, definitely."

When we reached the topmost window of the tower, I held onto Carly tightly with one arm, using the other to undo the latch and open the pane.

"Locks from the outside," she commented. "Yeah. Should have guessed that."

I climbed in, depositing her gently on the bed just as there was a knock at the door. "Enter," I announced.

The door opened and Khim rushed in, her ceremonial robes gathered up around her knees. She was the youngest healer ever to work at the Ruby Stronghold, and although she was immensely talented in her duties, she hadn't yet learned to move with the smooth, knowing, unhurried grace of her predecessors.

I appreciated that. I'd always felt there was a certain smugness, an arrogance and self-importance, in the serene way other healers walked. As though they had all the time in the world. As though they were so certain in their abilities that they'd be able to heal whatever they encountered, or else it was entirely past healing – either way, they seemed to feel there was no dignity in rushing to find out.

Personally, I felt that if someone had called for a healer, the situation was almost certainly an emergency, and haste was therefore required.

"Blood Ruler! I came as soon as I heard. Are you wounded?"

"No, but our guest is." I gestured to Carly, who was holding her arm at an odd angle to keep from bleeding on the sheets.

Khim seemed slightly taken aback by the identity of her new patient, but nevertheless, she wasted no time in crouching beside her to examine the arm and ankle. "Hmm. The abrasions are shallow, and there is some minor straining of the tendons in her lower extremity. She doesn't appear to be in any danger."

"Then would you please stop her bleeding?" I tried to keep the plaintive tone from my voice, with only marginal success.

A small smile played across Khim's lips, and for a moment, I thought she was going to make some flippant remark about how such a wound on a blood slave would ordinarily seem like an unexpected blessing – after all, Khim was known for being impertinent at times, even in situations when such behavior wasn't considered appropriate.

Instead, she nodded, reaching into the satchel she carried on her shoulder. "Certainly, Blood Ruler. This should only take a moment."

"Ugh, you're not going to give me stitches, are you?" Carly groaned. "I hate stitches."

Khim laughed. "No, we don't use *stitches* here on Valkred… nor do we rely on leeches, trepanning, or any other primitive Earthling medical practice. Honestly, stitches! The very idea!"

She removed a polished oval stone of blue marble hanging on a leather string, then held it just above Carly's arm, murmuring a few words in our native tongue. The cuts on Carly's arm glowed a corresponding shade of blue for a moment, and then the skin pulled itself together, healing rapidly. The last few rivulets of blood trickled down her skin, but their source had vanished completely.

"Thank you, Khim," I said.

She bowed. "I serve at your pleasure, Blood Ruler, as do we all. Would you like me to choose a… less-experienced healer from my coterie, to see to the needs of your… guest… in the future?"

I raised my eyebrows. "No, Khim, I believe you're quite suited to the task. Unless, of course, you feel that tending to the medical requirements of a human is somehow beneath the dignity of your station?"

"Not at all, Blood Ruler." She paused, then added impishly, "As long as I'm here, would you like me to scrub the blood stains from the sheets and the floor as well?"

I bared my fangs. "*That will be all, Khim.*"

She bowed again, making her exit without another word.

"She, um, doesn't seem to like me very much, does she?" Carly asked timidly. "But then again, I'm starting to feel like no one on this whole planet does."

"I like you," I replied briskly. "That is all that matters."

"Do you? Because sometimes, I'm not so sure."

I found myself momentarily at a loss for words. I cleared my throat, stalling. "Come. Let us adjourn to my bedchamber, until one of the palace servants has had a chance to properly clean yours." I had to get away from the bloodstains as soon as possible.

Carly hopped out of bed, following me across the hall. "I still can't believe she was able to just magically heal me like that. What was that stone thingy she was holding over me?"

"It was a Gem of Sy'Torak. They contain powerful healing energies, when properly polished and engraved. They're extremely rare – they're only bestowed upon Valkred who ascend to the level of Venerable Healer."

"Where do they come from?"

"We mine many precious gemstones from the caves beneath our planet's surface. Quite a few of them have fascinating properties. They're one of our primary sources of trade with other worlds and civilizations. Some have more minor healing or relaxing effects, some provide seemingly-endless sources of illumination, some power starships or have euphoric or intoxicating qualities."

"I'd love to see those mines someday. I'll bet they're beautiful, with all those clusters of magic jewels."

I smirked. "I can promise you, the reality of the mines is far less magical than what you might imagine. They're dark, dirty, dangerous places, filled with loud equipment for burrowing and processing the gems."

Carly pursed her lips. "In that case, I guess I'll skip it. If they're such nasty places to work, why would anyone want to? I mean, it can't just be that they need the money… you said poverty isn't really a thing on this planet."

"Miners, even low-level ones, are given great respect and deference in our society," I explained. "They are honored almost as highly as our warriors, due to their willingness to endanger themselves for the benefit of our economy." I paused, then added stiffly, "I… *do* like you, you know. I am sorry that we quarreled earlier. My behavior was inappropriate, under the circumstances. I've been under a tremendous amount of pressure of late, and it's put a strain on my temper. Which is, admittedly, a bit volatile to begin with."

"My, what a charming apology," Carly said with a grin. "That can't have been easy for you."

I chuckled. "No, I suppose not. In fairness, as Blood Ruler, I'm not often required to make apologies."

Even when I owe them to my own people, I thought bitterly, remembering Elrisa's treachery again. How it had almost cost us the war. The wounded, distrustful look that had begun to appear in the eyes of my subjects as a result whenever I ventured outside the Ruby Stronghold. *What if Torqa is right about Carly? What if I'm simply making the same damn mistake all over again?*

No. I couldn't force myself to believe, even for a moment, that Carly had been turned loose on me as some sort of living weapon, designed to take advantage of my trusting nature.

"Well, you're forgiven," Carly chirped, leaning forward to give me a kiss on the forehead. "And for the record, Akzun, you don't have any reason to be jealous where I'm concerned. You're the only Space Dracula for me."

I let out a hearty laugh. "I'm delighted to hear it. You seemed… quite friendly with Lun when I saw you together."

"Yeah, Lun's a cool guy. Funny, too. Mostly, I was just happy to be around flying machines again, you know? I miss it a lot. Getting up to my elbows in hot metal and grease, tinkering around, getting them back in the air. Hell, I missed it even *before* I got beamed up by a UFO."

I frowned. "*You* helped build space-faring vessels on Earth?"

"No, I came from the lower classes," she sighed. "We weren't allowed to get the kind of education it would have taken to learn how to work on spaceships. I was an airplane mechanic. Do you know what airplanes are?"

"Certainly. Primitive vehicles fueled by combustible chemicals, which are used for air travel despite being limited to your planet's lower atmosphere."

Carly nodded. "That about sums it up, I guess. I always saw them as more than that, though. To me, there was a certain beauty, a poetry to them."

"Really? How so?"

She thought it over for a moment. "A lot of reasons. Part of it was the joy, the anticipation, the adventure of traveling to another place. I was too poor to ever do that myself, but it was nice to know that my small contribution could help make it happen for other people. It felt like a gift I could give to the world, something that made me special."

"Based on our interactions – and the loveliness of your countenance – I find it extremely difficult to believe you've ever had any trouble feeling special."

Carly giggled. "Yeah? Well, if you really think so, you should visit Earth more often. On second thought, no, you probably shouldn't – they've seen too many monster movies there, they'd probably come after you with torches and pitchforks."

I touched her newly-healed arm gently. "I don't always understand the precise meaning of the things you say, Carly, but I enjoy the way you say them."

"Why, Blood Ruler, keep this up and I'll start to believe you're trying to seduce me," she said with a flirtatious wink.

That stopped me short. Am I? Yes, I suppose I am. Strange – she's already given herself to me physically, but now it seems I want more. I desire her trust, her admiration, her…

… Love?

Was that a word I was truly prepared to use where she was concerned? I wanted to simply give in and follow my instincts – but instead, the thought caused ripples of apprehension to spread through my soul, like a stone dropped in a pond.

I wasn't merely responsible for my own life, my own heart. I had the weight of an entire empire on my shoulders. What if my infatuation with her interfered with my duty to Valkred?

How could I live with myself if I failed my people again?

"Did you always want to work on air-planes?" I asked.

"Yeah, I suppose I did. My dad used to raise pigeons on the roof, and I loved the way they flew through the air. When I was a kid, I'd stay up there, watching them for hours. Wishing I could fly like they did." She paused, then said with a small grin, "Like *you* do. One time when I was six, I made a pair of wings for myself out of cardboard, with lots of paper feathers glued to them. I stood out in the front yard, flapping my arms, frustrated, wondering why it wasn't working. My dad laughed, then took me up to the pigeon coops to give me a closer look at the shape of their wings."

I couldn't help smiling at the image of this little version of Carly. "And what did you discover?"

"He explained how it wasn't just flapping that allowed them to soar like that. That it was something called the Bernoulli equation: Basically, an increase in velocity leads to a decrease in pressure, so the resulting liftoff is proportional to dynamic pressure and wing area." She laughed. "Now that I think about it, based on the lesson it's a good thing I didn't make a second attempt by jumping off the roof."

"Still, your understanding of such concepts at a young age must have been quite impressive," I pointed out. "Had you received an opportunity to continue your studies at a higher level, you might have been a member of the ruling classes, designing propulsion drives for long-range space flight."

"Right. Then I could've been one of the assholes responsible for selling people like me to people like you, right?" she said slyly.

I lowered my eyes. "You are correct in saying so, of course. I regret that I am forced to participate in a system such as that, which reduces capable women like you to helpless victims and livestock…"

"Relax, Akzun, I'm just yanking your chain a little. I may not love it, but I certainly understand it. It's hard to change the way things are, even for a Blood Ruler."

Relief washed over me. "Thank you. I am pleased that you comprehend my dilemma."

"No problem. Anyway," she went on, "sometimes I'd look up at the planes flying overhead, and I'd wonder how the hell those big metal tubes could ever get off the ground. When I learned that they worked on the same principle as the pigeons' wings, I decided I wanted to find out everything I could about them. So I became an airplane mechanic. Until I lost my job."

"How did that happen? Surely, with a mind such as yours, you performed your duties admirably."

"Damn right I did." There was an edge to her voice.

"Then why…?"

"My supervisor didn't care how well I did my work. He just wanted to treat me like I was his personal plaything."

"Yes, I can see how that would be a problem, given how strong-willed you are," I said with a chuckle. "What did you do to put off his advances?"

"I told him to fuck off, and when he didn't get the message, I kicked him in the balls."

I burst out laughing. "In that case, I suppose I owe you a great debt of gratitude for not giving me the same treatment."

"Well, it didn't hurt that you're a lot more handsome than he was," she answered, looking up at me through her eyelashes, teasing. "Besides, just before we met, it was explained to me that not all species carry their genitals in the same place, so there was no guarantee it'd be as effective in your case."

"I see. And now that you're confident in the location of my… balls, as you call them?"

She made a great show of thinking it over. "I'm not particularly inclined to kick them. Not yet, anyway. As long as you stay in line."

I bowed. "Your forbearance is greatly appreciated."

"You're welcome." She yawned. "Ugh, it feels like I haven't really rested at all since I first got here. Do you think the servants are done cleaning up the blood in my chamber yet?"

"I am not sure. However," I added tentatively, "you may certainly sleep in here with me. If you wish."

She slipped under the sheets, then shed her trousers, tossed them on the floor, and curled up next to me, nodding. "Thanks. I'd like that…"

Then her voice trailed off, and she was asleep, her comforting warmth pressed against my side.

Chapter Fifteen

Carly

I have no idea how long I was conked out, but my sleep was deep and dreamless, and I woke up feeling incredibly refreshed. There were a few pale rays of purplish sunlight shining through the window – the first ones I'd seen since coming to Valkred.

I yawned and stretched, rolling over to find Akzun looking at me. There was amusement and tenderness in his intense eyes… and desire, too.

He reached out to stroke my cheek with his cold fingers. "Good morning. Are you rested?"

"Yes, very. Thank you." I giggled.

He tilted his head to the side curiously. "Why do you laugh?"

I shook my head. "Whether you're on Earth or in a galaxy far, far away, there's one absolute constant to the universe, it seems."

"Oh? What is that?"

"When you wake up to find a guy looking at you the way you're looking at me right now," I explained, climbing on top of him and straddling him playfully, "you can bet there's only one thing on his mind."

I leaned down, kissing him passionately. His tongue sought mine out eagerly, and he put his hands on my hips, stroking my thighs and buttocks. God, his touch was amazing. Once he got started, I couldn't get enough of it.

"Do you wish to open your mind to me again?"

I thought about it, then shook my head, remembering the mixed messages and unpleasant aftermath of our last lovemaking session. "Let's keep things physical this time, okay? Less complicated that way."

He nodded, but seemed vaguely disappointed. "Very well. If that is what you prefer."

"Hey, don't worry," I said, planting a kiss on the tip of his nose. "There's plenty of other things I'm willing to open to you."

Akzun smiled, and it occurred to me how few times I'd seen that expression on him since meeting him. It seemed to light up his handsome features, making him less intimidating, more approachable and relatable. Come to think of it, that's probably why he doesn't do it much.

I felt his hard cock between my legs, and it made my pussy wetter than it had ever been before. The first time had been… well, the first time. I hadn't known what to expect from sex with an alien – one who'd bought me as a slave, at that. I hadn't known whether I'd like the experience, whether I'd even be physically capable of enjoying it, given the differences in our anatomies. Fear had tainted the build-up, even though I hadn't fully acknowledged that to myself at the time.

This time, though, I knew what I was in for, and I couldn't wait.

I shucked off my shirt, threw it aside, then rubbed my pelvis against his, relishing the deep, throaty moan it elicited from him. His entire body was quivering – I could feel how much he wanted me, his desire coming off him in thick, sultry waves, like the heat of a fever.

I put my hands behind my head. The gesture lifted my breasts slightly, and I liked the way his eyes focused on them hungrily.

"Do you want me, Akzun?" I teased.

"Yes." His voice was hoarse, barely above a whisper.

I went up on my knees, keeping my crotch tantalizingly out of reach from his. "Tell me how much."

He took a deep breath, lifting his hips, desperately trying to push against me again. "More than I've ever wanted anyone, Carly. More than I've ever wanted anything in my life."

"Good." I lowered myself again, and oh, he was throbbing so *hard!* I could practically take his pulse just from the feel of his cock against my thigh. "Then I'm yours."

We were rubbing against each other so hard that my juices were almost churning into a lather. He reached up, crossing his powerful arms behind my back and pulling me down so we were face to face – just as, with the same motion, he plunged inside of me.

"Oh my God," I breathed out slowly, loving the way his shaft felt between the lips of my pussy – the way he filled me up relentlessly, deeper and deeper, until he felt like a hard, thick, beautiful icicle piercing all the way to my core.

He cradled my face in his cold hands, staring into my eyes, through them, into my heart. Our bodies rocked together, back and forth, his thrusts steadily becoming more insistent.

"Are you truly mine, Carly?"

"Yes."

"Then say it again," he demanded.

I opened my mouth, but at first, nothing would come out except a lusty sigh. It was as though my thoughts were radio signals, and his intensity was scrambling them before I could manage to shape them into anything coherent.

Suddenly, he stopped thrusting, holding my face more tightly. "Tell me," he growled through clenched teeth, "or I'll stop."

Then the words came tumbling from my lips. "I'm yours, Akzun, oh God, baby, I'm *yours*, I'm *so fucking yours.* Please, *please, don't stop…*"

He grinned, plunging himself inside me again. "Good. Don't ever forget that you're mine."

"I won't, baby, I promise…"

His palms were pressed against my back so hard I was sure they'd leave bruises there, but I didn't care. I wanted him to hold me as tightly as he could. I wanted to feel his need for me, to be locked in this embrace with him forever. His skin was blissfully chilly against mine, brisk and refreshing, quenching my bottomless thirst for him.

Our hearts were quickening, their rhythms thrumming together until it felt like they were beating as one. I was so close, ready to go over the edge – and I could feel that he was, too.

"Come for me," I begged. "Please, I need to feel you."

His back arched sharply and he climaxed, a cool gush to put out the fire raging through me. I shook and spasmed, screamed and slammed against him, my orgasm blossoming up my spine and into my brain like a series of explosions.

Then we were side by side on the sheets, holding each other and nuzzling happily.

"Hey, it's daytime," I pointed out. "Aren't you going to shrivel up or burst into flames in the sun or something? Do you need to, like, go sleep in a coffin in the dungeons or something?"

He laughed. "I don't make a habit of sleeping down there, no. And it seems as though you keep forgetting that the stories of so-called vampires on your world have little to do with the realities of my race."

"Still, it makes me wonder," I mused. "How long have the Valkred been visiting Earth? Stealing blood slaves, all that?"

Akzun gave it some thought. "We've only started formally visiting your world relatively recently – within the past hundred years or so. On the other hand, the practice of periodically abducting human blood slaves goes back almost as far as the earliest recorded history of our Modern Age. Given the voyages of our first deep-space explorers, I suppose it's entirely possible that we first came upon your planet… oh, several thousand years ago, perhaps."

"See, that would make sense," I continued, "because it'd probably explain how vampire legends first started on Earth, and why every culture has them, in one form or another. So tell me, when was *The Tale of Cyrus and Skorpona* written?"

He blinked at me, surprised. "I assume Zark provided you with that particular book, to help you pass the time while I was away?"

I nodded.

"Ha. That was rather clever of him. It was a favorite of mine when I was a small child. And no doubt you recognized certain… parallels, between that story and our situation?"

"Kind of hard not to, right?"

"He probably meant it as a form of encouragement for you, in his own strange way. Not to mention a joke on me. Just because something has been written in a work of fiction, though, doesn't mean it's not still taboo in real life," he pointed out.

"True. But at least it means it's not unheard of, either. And besides, if it was your favorite book as a kid, maybe that's true of other Valkred as well."

"Ah. So you believe their sense of childish romance will overcome their sense of cultural propriety?"

"Hey, I'm just saying maybe our situation, as you put it, isn't quite so hopeless after all," I said. "Maybe your people are ready for a change."

"That's precisely what I fear," he countered. "That they will be ready for a change of Blood Ruler, if I manage to sufficiently displease them."

"Well, either way, it's far too early for pessimism. What shall we do today? No, wait… I guess I'm probably on my own again for a while, right? You've got war stuff to deal with."

He snickered. "Torqa and Zark are hard at work, trying to find the traitors in our midst before M'ruvev's deadline elapses. There's nothing for me to do about it personally except fret and pace the halls until I receive news from them. And as for the rest of my duties as Blood Ruler, I happen to have a sizable and capable staff to deal with such matters. So no, I do not believe I will, in fact, focus my energies on *war stuff* today. As you said, it is too early in the day to brood with such dark thoughts. I believe I shall spend my time with you instead, if you would find that agreeable. Or would you prefer to browse other novels by the same author? I do not think they would be to your taste… the story of Cyrus and Skorpona was the only work of hers that was not a tragedy."

"Hmm. Yeah, no, not in the mood for tragedies today," I said with a giggle. "I'd love to spend the day with you. What did you have in mind? Besides the obvious, of course." I bumped my hips against his side a few times suggestively.

Akzun stroked my hair, brushing a strand of it from my face. "You've spoken of your love for flying machines. Would you care to pilot my ship?"

My eyes widened. "That would be awesome! I didn't get to spend too much time crawling around in your shuttle, but the controls seemed relatively simple. I'm pretty sure I could –"

"No, no, not the shuttle," he said with a grin. "My ship. The Angel's Wrath."

I couldn't believe it. "Wow. I mean… wow. You'd really trust me to do that?"

"Not without my supervision, of course." He chuckled. "We wouldn't want you accidentally bombing the capitol city. Or choosing the wrong setting on the propulsion drive and finding yourself in Mana territory, or stranded at the galactic rim. But yes, Carly, I would trust you with my ship. In many ways, I've already trusted you with far more than that."

"Then let's do it!" I hopped out of bed, grabbing my clothes and pulling them on. "I can't wait!"

"Can't wait for what, human?" an all-too-familiar voice asked coldly.

I turned and saw Torqa standing in the doorway with a sour expression.

"Certainly, you can't seriously believe that Akzun intends to allow you to pilot the flagship of the Valkred fleet," she went on, sauntering in and circling the bed slowly. "What a foolish notion. He was joking, naturally. He would never grant you access to that vessel's secure databanks or weapons systems. He would never demonstrate such a grievous lapse of judgment, or compromise the security of our military in such an egregious manner. No, he was amusing himself at your expense, surely."

"I was *not* joking, Torqa," Akzun snarled, "any more than I was joking when I told you what would happen the next time you entered the palace uninvited."

"Oh? Then follow through on your threats, O Most Esteemed and Infallible Blood Ruler!" Torqa sneered. "Go on! Call the guards! Have them take me to the Detention Center and strap me into my own interrogation cube! Order my execution! I would find that fate preferable to standing here and watching the leader of the Valkred mewl and play and have his tummy rubbed like some weak little Jenka cub, all while his own people are in danger! At least I'd have the pleasure of knowing that before I died, I'd seen you act like a real man, a real Blood Ruler, instead of a helpless, addled, lovesick imbecile!"

"Jesus, Akzun, you let this bitch talk to you like that?" I asked.

"Yes, he does let me talk to him like that, because what else is he going to do?" Torqa spat. "Attempt to find the traitors among our people *himself?* Arrest them, torture them to their breaking points, carry out their death sentences? No, he could never do that in such a time of crisis, because *that* would require *a genuine show of strength!*"

"If you're so certain that you are the only one truly capable of carrying out these tasks," Akzun replied, "then perhaps you should be out there doing so, instead of standing in your leader's bedchamber and hurling inane insults at him. Meanwhile, if I choose to allow Carly to pilot the Angel's Wrath, that is my privilege."

"So you've unilaterally decided, then, that she is not a threat to our interests? That she couldn't *possibly* be a spy or saboteur, that there's absolutely no chance of that whatsoever? You've arrived at that decision conclusively, have you?"

"Yes," Akzun answered. "As a matter of fact, I have."

"Well, then I suppose we must all bow before your impeccable judgment, eh? After all, it's not as though you've ever made these sorts of mistakes before."

"Torqa," Akzun said dangerously through gritted teeth, "you go too far. And just because you believe yourself to be comfortably above reprimand during wartime does *not* mean the same will hold true once we are at peace, or that your insults will go unremembered. I would urge you to seriously consider that before you choose your next words."

She opened her mouth, closed it, then opened it again. "I will take my leave of you now, Blood Ruler, so that you may… *indulge* yourself as you see fit. I only hope that when I attempt to contact you regarding our search for the traitors, you will make yourself available, regardless of what you happen to be in the middle of," she finished, eyeing me with distaste.

And with that, she opened the window, hopped onto the sill, spread her wings, and flew away.

Akzun turned to me, raising an eyebrow. "Why can't you kick *her* in the balls, hmm?"

I was about to laugh, then stopped myself. "Do… do the females on this world *have* balls?"

He cackled loudly, but I could see in the set of his shoulders that he was more unsettled than he wanted to let on. "Come, we won't let that harpy spoil our morning. Let's hop in the shuttle and take you up to the Angel's Wrath. We keep it docked on an orbital platform."

He led me out to the landing pad on the grounds, and we lifted off in the shuttle, the blue-purple atmosphere of Valkred swiftly giving way to the inky blackness of space. Sure enough, there was a small space station with a flat surface waiting for us in orbit. It was surrounded by an array of floating automated cannons the size of cars, and the cone-shaped flagship was docked on top of it.

Akzun punched some keys on the shuttle's console and we quickly caught up with the platform. The cannons aimed at us for a few ominous seconds, but their sensors must have recognized the Blood Ruler's private vessel, because they pointed away again sharply.

A large door slid open on top of the Angel's Wrath, revealing the shuttle bay. We lowered ourselves into it with a series of deft maneuvers, and once the door shut again above us and the atmosphere inside was restored, we climbed out. The inside of the bay was a perfect rectangle of black marble threaded with crimson.

He led me to what looked like a smooth, uninterrupted wall, standing in front of it. As I watched, several sections of the wall shifted and slid, revealing a doorway. I followed him through it, looking around and taking in my surroundings. The last time I was aboard this flagship, I'd been newly bought by Akzun, and I was angry and frightened out of my wits.

This time, I was eager to properly appreciate it.

Akzun may have joked about not sleeping in a coffin like the vampires in Earth literature, but as we walked through the empty corridors together, I couldn't help but notice how much the décor reminded me of a funeral casket. The surfaces appeared to be polished black wood, with brass fixtures like the handles on a coffin, and certain areas were upholstered with what looked like red velvet.

The air was kept chilled, which wasn't a surprise, and the lights were set to a low level. The gloom that filled the corners and crept in on all sides made me extremely uneasy, but when I edged closer to Akzun, I felt better.

It was funny. As a kid, I was afraid of monsters in the dark. Now I was clinging to the arm of a vampire, hoping he'd keep me safe.

We stepped onto the flight deck, and I ran my hands over the control consoles lightly – remembering how hard I'd tried to study them during the trip from Cexeia to Valkred, desperately trying to plot my escape by any means necessary.

Well, now I was about to learn how to operate them. Armed with that information, would I still try to find a way home if a chance presented itself?

It was hard to imagine that I would, but if it came to it, I couldn't really be sure.

I was enjoying Akzun's company more than I'd ever liked any male companionship I'd found on Earth. I had an entire galaxy of wonder and adventure at my fingertips. New foods, new creatures, new experiences. Yes, there seemed to be plenty of dangers out here in space – but Earth was pretty unsafe, too, for people like me in the lower classes. Gangs roamed the streets after dark, robbing and attacking people. Homes were broken into regularly, looted and vandalized. There was disease, poverty, starvation. And in the end, did it matter if the assholes who sneered and postured and threw their weight around had fangs like Torqa or fat guts and grabby hands like Lars?

But Earth was still my home. Deep down, there was still some part of me that hoped to see it again someday.

Yeah, that'll work out real well. I'll just show up one day in my old neighborhood, in a big-ass spaceship. "Hey, guys, check out my new ride! Isn't it sweet? Check out the bass on the stereo system. My alien boyfriend gave it to me. Oh, yeah, by the way, aliens are totally a thing, and so are vampires, and they're actually the same thing a lot of the time. Hey, wait, what's going on? What's with all the crosses and garlic…?"

I snorted with laughter.

"What's so funny?" Akzun asked.

"Oh, nothing. Just thinking about what would happen if they could see me now."

"Who?"

I shrugged. "Everyone. So, should we take this thing out for a spin, or what?"

He motioned toward the command chair. "The basic controls have been re-routed to your console. By all means, have a seat."

I sat down, feeling a big, goofy grin on my face. I couldn't help it. All those hours, months, years, working on airplanes I'd never be allowed to ride in, let alone pilot…

And today, I was going to fly a fucking spaceship.

Chapter Sixteen

Akzun

"All right, now change course and engage the left rear thrusters," I said, leaning over the back of the command chair and watching Carly enter commands on the console. "Don't forget to adjust the stabilizers accordingly."

"What, like this?"

She punched in a key sequence and the ship lurched to one side. I stumbled, smacking my shoulder against a bulkhead and wincing.

"Are you all right?" she asked, running over to me.

"No, no, stay in the command chair!" I cried out. "You have to correct course, or else we'll –"

Too late.

The Angel's Wrath did a full barrel roll, the ceiling switching places with the floor just long enough for us to plummet and bump our heads. Carly let out a sharp squeal of panic. When we came right-side up again, I grabbed her and spread my wings – the quarters were a bit too close for real flying, but at least I was able to catch her before her head smacked against the hard surface once more.

Still, we both came down hard on our backsides, our brief plummet barely cushioned by my feathers.

We looked at each other and laughed.

"Okay, so you should probably teach me how not to do that again," she said, rubbing her forehead. "Because seriously, *ow*."

"That little misadventure aside, you're learning very quickly," I reassured her, carrying her back to the command seat. "You have the basic thruster controls. They simply require a bit more… finesse, ha."

"Finesse. Right. Got it. Even so, though, I'm starting to see why it usually takes a full crew to fly this damn thing."

I shook my head. "Most of the crew assigned to the flagship are warriors, meant to guard me during travels and diplomatic missions. The ones on the command deck are useful, to be sure, but their presence is largely ceremonial. They're mostly meant to act as redundancies – if one pilot is out of commission, another can take his place, and another, and so on, until the vessel can be flown by a single person: the Blood Ruler himself."

"But is there ever a circumstance where that would really be necessary?" Carly asked. "Where the Blood Ruler would have to fly the ship alone?"

"Yes. If the fleet is up against a superior foe with no hope of survival, it is customary for the Blood

Ruler to dismiss all crew to the escape pods, ignite the engine core, and manually pilot the Angel's Wrath directly at the enemy, at ramming speed. The impact and explosion might be enough to destroy them, or at least enough of their forces to allow the remaining Valkred to rally against them and win."

"You'd really be expected to do that?" Carly asked, wide-eyed. "Stay aboard while everyone else bailed out, and sacrifice yourself?"

"It's the only course of action under such circumstances."

"But I mean, you guys have such advanced technology. Isn't there some way to just set it to auto-pilot instead?"

"It is not a question of technology," I explained. "It is a matter of honor. A Blood Ruler who has led his people into such a hopeless scenario must acknowledge his own failure – his poor judgment and leadership – and atone for it accordingly. Besides, do you not have a similar protocol on your world? What is the saying… 'The captain must go down with his ship?'"

"Yeah, we kind of outgrew that way of thinking a while ago."

"You outgrew honor," I chuckled. "How convenient for you."

She looked over the console for a long moment, lost in thought. Finally, she asked, "What about, um, weapons? How do those work?"

I raised an eyebrow. "Why do you want to know? Are you envisioning some scenario in which you manage to steal my flagship, bravely pilot it back to your home world, and fire upon any who might try to stop you?"

Am I truly joking? A shadow passed over my heart like the silhouette of a predator falling over its prey. Or is this an outcome I'm genuinely anxious about? I thought I'd dismissed Torqa's accusations as baseless paranoia and jealousy…but why is Carly interested in weaponry?

"No, nothing like that," she said. "Just… what if there's a space battle, and something happens to the guy in charge of the firing systems, and I need to take over the controls?"

"If there is indeed a *space battle*," I replied, "I highly doubt that you will be aboard this ship. But if it will make you happy to learn, then by all means."

I set a new course in the navigational computer, then programmed the weapons systems to be routed through the command controls. The ship glided off to its updated destination, the orbital docking platform quickly fading into the distance behind us.

"Where are we going?" she asked.

"To a location more ideal for target practice." I waited for the new location to appear on the view screen before us, then cut the engines.

I'd brought us to a stationary asteroid belt surrounding a moon at the far edge of the Valkred system.

"This," I began, pointing out a set of controls, "is your targeting system. This button fires concussive pulse mortars – either singularly or in a tight barrage, depending on the setting – while that one controls the plasma disruptors. You may choose an asteroid, pretend that it's Torqa, and fire at will."

Carly laughed. "That's one hell of an incentive to shoot straight. But what if I miss and hit the surface of that moon? Am I going to hit any colonies, or blast it out of orbit and change the tides of the planet it's orbiting, or anything like that?"

"There are no lunar colonies out here for you to worry about. And while I might wish our weapons systems were powerful enough to blast an entire moon out of its orbit, I can assure you they are not. Well, not *this* moon, at any rate."

"Fair enough. Here… we… go." She keyed in a target, and the crosshairs appeared on the view screen.

She hit the button – and a pulse mortar discharged from one of the tubes beneath the ship, careening toward a large asteroid. It went off-center, nicking the side of the giant rock and sending it spinning off away from the rest of the field.

"Not bad for a first attempt," I said admiringly. "Keep this up, and we might make a halfway decent tactical officer out of you yet."

"Yeah, but then I'd have to join the Valkred military," she replied uncertainly. "Which would mean you'd finally have to let me carry a blaster, like the one you've got on your belt there."

I looked at her for a long moment, then reached over and hit a button. The view screen cut off.

"What is it, Akzun? Did I say something wrong?"

I stood directly in front of the command chair, staring down at her sternly. "Carly, why are you suddenly so curious about weapons?"

She shifted in her seat uncomfortably. "I guess that's probably making you kind of nervous, huh? I'm sorry. I shouldn't have said anything."

"Perhaps not, but you haven't answered my question."

Carly took a deep breath, closing her eyes for a moment. When she opened them, she said, "I think you know how I feel about you, Akzun. We haven't been together very long, but… I'm… I don't know, *drawn* to you. I like being with you. I like your castle. Even Valkred is starting to grow on me, despite all the cold and the darkness. And I know you care about me, and that you wouldn't hurt me. You haven't even sucked out any of my blood yet, and I know how much you paid to do that to me, so it means a lot. But I'm still just a human. I'm still about a zillion light-years from the only planet I've ever known. I'm surrounded by things I don't understand, some of which could seriously hurt me or worse. Half the aliens I've met seem to want to kill the other half, and then there's all of Torqa's sneering and threats – she just seems to step out of the shadows whenever it suits her like some kind of ghost, you know? And she *hates* me. In fact, if I understand the situation correctly, a *lot* of people on your world hate me, and even the ones who *don't* would drink me dry if they had a chance. I don't have wings to fly away from them, or fangs to defend myself."

"I will protect you," I assured her. "I will keep you from harm, I swear it."

"I know you want to, Akzun, and I know you'll try. But you're the Blood Ruler. You've got an entire planet to lead, not to mention a war to win. You can't be with me every moment."

I thought this over. I hated to admit it – I didn't want to accept the idea that I couldn't guarantee her safety, even from a distance – but she had a point. When it came right down to it, I couldn't even be entirely sure that my own palace guards would have her best interests at heart. What if one of them was affected by the bloodlust? For that matter, what if Torqa managed to gain their loyalty through bribes or blackmail?

"You're right," I sighed, unclipping my blaster from my belt and handing it to her. "You should be able to defend yourself if the need ever arises."

"Thanks." She attached it to the side of her pants. Despite its weight, the material stayed in place.

"I will instruct you on how to use it properly as well," I told her. "There's a firing range here on the ship that we can use."

But her words had given me another idea as well – one I took some time to ponder as she studiously learned the firing controls for the Wrath's weapon systems.

The past week had no doubt been extremely overwhelming for her. Abruptly taken from her home world and everything she knew, forced to serve drinks and endure the abuse of that odious troll Nos, bought by me as a slave, intimidated by Torqa, nearly flattened by a falling statue – it would have been enough to drive anyone in the galaxy utterly mad, or at least jangle their nerves beyond repair.

And still, she'd handled it better than anyone else would. She'd shown courage, resourcefulness, determination, strength of will, even a sense of humor.

Shouldn't she be rewarded for demonstrating such astounding resilience? Didn't she deserve a chance to relax, to get away from it all for a while and recover after enduring so many severe shocks to the system?

Yes, of course.

But I also knew there was more to it than that.

I wanted a chance for us to enjoy each other's company without any outside stressors or interference. I wanted to see where it would take us – whether we'd genuinely be good together if given the opportunity, or if all of this had simply been a momentary fluke of passion and circumstance.

"Would you please pardon me for a moment?" I asked her, getting up to leave. "I'll be back shortly."

"Well, okay, but are you sure you trust me to be around all these pulse mortars and plasma whatevers without any supervision?"

I smiled. "Certainly. Just try not to get us into any more intergalactic wars while I'm gone."

"I'm not making any promises." She laughed, returning to the firing controls and singling out another large asteroid.

I went to my quarters, activated my private communications console, and contacted Zark. His holographic visage appeared immediately.

"So, brother, I heard you took Carly for a little pleasure cruise on the Angel's Wrath?" he joked.

"In a manner of speaking. Actually, I wanted to speak with you about that. But first: Have you had any luck with the Mana?"

He sighed. "I've been using back channels, naturally, but that'll only get me so far. There are plenty of groups who'd want to get the war going again. Some of them are believed to have Valkred spies reporting to them, while others are known to have access to the resources it would take to pose as Valkred and infiltrate our military. But concrete proof? Specific suspects to pursue?" He shrugged. "It's all just guesswork so far."

"I understand. Do your best, Zark. I have faith in your ability to get to the bottom of this fiasco."

"That makes one of us. Now, what did you want to talk to me about? No, wait, don't tell me: You want your brother's advice on how to properly satisfy a woman in bed."

"No, but thank you for putting *that* charming image in my head," I said with a grimace. "I'm planning to take some time with Carly. To… get away for a couple of days."

He blinked, surprised. "You are our Blood Ruler, and you may do as you wish in such matters, of course."

"But…?" I prodded.

"*But* your people might see this as proof that you'd rather go gadding about with your new blood slave than take the Mana threat seriously. *But* M'ruvev's people might goad him into using your sudden departure as an excuse to throw the deadline out the window and launch a full-scale assault. *But* you'd be leaving your brother and Torqa in charge – and frankly, there are plenty of Valkred who don't believe either one is up to the task, myself included."

"Yes, yes. Other than that, though, what do you think of the idea?"

Zark grinned. "Other than that, I think you deserve some relaxation with this woman you're so fond of, and I hope you have a marvelous trip."

"Thank you, Zark. And for what it's worth: I have every confidence that you are up to the task of ruling Valkred in my absence."

"You do?"

"Don't be ridiculous, of course not. But what do you expect me to say? That our planet would be better off with a mentally defective Drekkir toddler sitting on the throne?"

He smirked. "You're all heart, brother. I hope she gives you an incurable case of Aldivian genital rot."

I cut off the communication, laughing. Then I returned to the flight deck.

"Carly, I have something to tell you."

"Wait! Before you do, take a look at the view screen."

I peered at it, trying to make out what I was supposed to see. There was a massive asteroid in the center of the screen – its surface was scored with plasma marks, and smoke and debris were drifting from it.

"A direct hit!" I crowed. "Well done! Most impressive!"

"You haven't seen the impressive part yet," she said. "Hang on just a sec while I zoom in, and..."

The asteroid was magnified onscreen, and when I saw what she was referring to, my eyes widened in disbelief.

She had used the most narrow setting on the plasma beam to engrave the rock with the initials A and C – and to sketch a crude Earthling representation of a heart around them.

"Just a little something to commemorate our first voyage together," she said proudly.

I was so deeply touched that for a moment, I couldn't find any words. "Thank you, Carly. That was… tremendously thoughtful of you."

"Well, thank *you* for treating me like more than just another blood slave."

"Carly, I wanted to ask: How would you feel about just staying out here among the stars with me for a couple of days? We can go anywhere we like, and forget about Torqa and the Mana for a while. Would you like that?"

"That sounds wonderful," she replied hesitantly, "but are you sure it's a good idea? With everything that's going on, can you really afford to just zoom off for a while like that?"

"If the Blood Ruler of Valkred says it's a good idea," I proclaimed stoically, "then it *is* a good idea."

She giggled. "Hey, who am I to argue with the King of the Space Vampires, right?"

Suddenly, her stomach growled loudly. She put a hand over it, wincing. "Oh, God, now *that's* embarrassing."

"Not at all. The body behaves as it behaves – there is no shame in it," I reassured her. "Do you require food?"

"Now that you mention it, I am pretty hungry. After all, my meal last night got interrupted by a falling statue. And by, you know… other things."

"Fair point. I must confess, I often forget that the members of your species require sustenance on a far more regular basis than we do. Come, let's get you to the galley so that you may eat."

"Is there a cook on board? I thought we were alone on the ship."

"We are. But the food storage units are always fully stocked. And before I went to live in the Ruby Stronghold with all of its chefs and servants, I was known for being rather capable in the kitchen myself," I added with a touch of pride.

"Oh, really? Well, I guess I'd better prepare to be impressed, then! Lead the way, Chef Akzun!"

Chapter Seventeen

Carly

I sat at a counter, watching Akzun move around the kitchen and prepare our meal. I was surprised – I had to admit, he seemed quite deft and knowledgeable as he modulated the cooking temperatures of the various stoves and surfaces and mixed the ingredients.

"So, what are we having?" I asked. "Whatever you're making, it smells heavenly."

"Thank you," he replied with a smile. "For your dining pleasure this evening, I have selected some of the finest delicacies the galaxy has to offer. Seared Clench-Mollusks from the oceanic depths of the Mana home world, which have been brining in their own juices since before the war – they should be immensely tender and succulent by now. A rare flank of ganjiibeast, packed in salt and Krote sweet spices. A loaf of bread baked from wheat harvested on the moonlit plains of Yuluna, and infused with nectars from the ancient clicker-bee hives on Nanryr. And pickled stems of thresher-daisies from the fourth moon of Xehrul, aged in a barrel of blood-beetle husks for flavor and then breaded with the powdered bone of sacrificial Drekkir demon-hounds."

I catalogued these improbable-sounding items in my head, then smiled. "You made some of those up, didn't you?"

Akzun met my gaze for a long moment, his expression unreadable – then broke into a wide grin. "Yes. That last dish I mentioned was indeed fictional. The rest are quite real, though. However, I *do* have something special to offer you. Something exceptionally rare."

He reached into a cabinet beneath the counter and produced a wine bottle, handing it to me. The words on the label appeared to be in French, and I read them aloud, certain that I was mangling the pronunciation horribly: "*1811 Chateau D'Yquem?*"

He nodded proudly. "A most expensive and sought-after bottle of wine. Its worth is estimated at over thirty thousand of your Earth dollars."

"Wow." I put it down on the counter quickly, filled with a dreadful certainty that if I didn't, I'd end up dropping it and breaking it by accident. "Where did you get this?"

"One of your planet's more, shall we say, ostentatious rulers collects such items, and presented it to me during my last visit as a sign of respect. Or fear, perhaps. With your people, it is sometimes difficult to tell for sure. Whenever I'm there, the look in their eyes tells me that I bear a certain resemblance to creatures from their nightmares, and that they would offer me anything just to quell their terror of me."

"Can't say I blame them," I said. "You spend your whole life having people tell you that vampires aren't real, and then one day, you're face to face with one. Besides, they aren't acquainted with your charming side like I am."

His face lit up in a way I'd never seen before. "What a lovely thing to say. Here, let's sample this treasure, shall we?" He removed a pair of glasses from a shelf, uncorked the wine, and poured it.

As I took a sip, I had to wonder: Was it my imagination, or had his behavior toward me changed significantly ever since my near miss with the statue in the garden? During our initial interactions, he had seemed so guarded and aloof, so imperious. But now he seemed open and engaging, unafraid to show his emotions. Was there anything specific I'd done to put him more at ease?

Or was he just… warming up to me, slowly and in his own way?

I couldn't say for sure, but whatever the reason, I liked it a lot and hoped it would continue. When he dropped the whole Blood Ruler routine and acted like a real person, it made me feel like I might be able to fall in love with him – to have a future with him, no matter what the rest of the Valkred felt about me being a human instead of one of them.

When we'd made love for the first time, he'd let a stray thought slip about making me his mate. But what did that mean to him? What did that mean for me? The term was such a strange one – so formal, almost clinical, the way the narrators on the Discovery Channel used to refer to animals that procreated. Surely, to the Valkred, it meant more than that? It meant something deeper, a real connection?

Was love even a concept on their world? For that matter, was marriage? I hadn't found any direct references to either in the novel Zark gave me, but then, it had been translated from its original language, so I wasn't sure I could rely on that for accuracy in this context.

Most of all, how was I supposed to even broach these topics without it seeming weird, presumptuous, or premature? Now that Akzun was loosening up around me, I didn't want to make him uncomfortable or withdrawn again.

"Akzun," I began, trying to sound casual, "have you ever had a mate before?"

He paused midway through cutting the ganjiibeast into chilled slivers. A shadow passed over his face, and I worried that I'd brought up some terrible memory for him.

"Yes. Her name was Elrisa. She… died."

"I'm so sorry to hear that. Do you mind me asking what happened? I mean, if you don't want to talk about it, that's okay."

He inhaled deeply, steeling himself. "No. I do not *wish* to talk about it. But I must. You have a right to know about her. About what happened. It will… clarify things for you somewhat, I believe."

I frowned, remembering the earlier interaction in Akzun's chamber. "Does this have anything to do with what Torqa was saying before we left?"

"I fear it does, yes."

"She said something about your judgment. About you 'making these kinds of mistakes before.' Was Elrisa some kind of spy?"

Akzun nodded sadly, focusing on the food and refusing to meet my gaze. "When I first saw her, it was at the Vukkovka Festival of Midnight. She was… the most beautiful member of my race I had ever laid eyes on. She was so perfect in her seduction. Our eyes met, and she gave me the smallest smile – but she did not approach me. She kept her distance and waited patiently for me to make the first move, for me to believe that *I* was the one in control of it all. She manipulated me. Expertly."

"It almost sounds like you admire her," I commented.

"And why not? It is no small thing to make a fool of the Blood Ruler of the Valkred." He paused, then added, "Or at least, it shouldn't be. There are those, like Torqa, who would say I made it quite easy for her."

"That's not fair."

"Isn't it?" Now there was a hard, bitter edge to his voice. "Oh, I made such a grand spectacle of our romance. I had chosen my consort, the perfect woman to sit by my side, to help represent our people to the rest of the galaxy. Lovely, graceful, well-mannered, and *so* devoted to me. *So* loving, *so* eager to please. She was everything I had ever wanted in a mate. I was positive that my people would adore her as much as I did."

"And did they?"

"For a while. Until the truth came out. Because no matter how much I loved her – no matter how many times I begged Torqa to embrace her as I did – my Supreme Advisor simply refused to trust her. Perhaps she was more perceptive than I was. Perhaps she saw something in Elrisa that I hadn't, something that made her suspect. Or perhaps she was acting out of pure jealousy, I don't know. But Torqa kept digging and digging, until she found exactly what she was looking for: proof that Elrisa had been using her relationship with me to collect crucial military information, and then transmitting it to the Mana."

"You must have been so heartbroken," I whispered.

"Heartbreak is a terrible thing," he said. "Heartbreak comes to all people who allow themselves to love, sooner or later. Heartbreak is a fact of life, like illness and death. But this was so much worse. I lost the trust, the *respect*, of my people. I'd made fools of us all. I'd made us look weak and gullible in front of the entire damn cosmos."

"So you had to have her executed," I guessed. "Or else you'd have been ousted by your people."

"I wanted to have her executed, yes. I wanted it to be something simple, private, and as painless as possible. I knew she had to die for her crimes, of course, but there was still some awful part of me that loved her. That refused to believe she was evil at her core, even after she confessed to her deeds. A part of me that didn't want her to suffer needlessly." He scowled. "Torqa talked me out of all that. She convinced me that the only way for me to remain in the Ruby Stronghold – the only way for me to avoid open revolt and attempts at assassination – was to make an example of Elrisa in the most gruesome way imaginable. She said she knew I didn't have the heart to do it myself. She said she'd take care of everything so I wouldn't have to. And she did. By the stars, she did. And it was…"

He swallowed hard, forcing himself to go on.

"The way Elrisa looked the last time I saw her – burned and bleeding, croaking and starving and pathetic – is something I still see in my nightmares to this day. To be honest, Carly, it terrifies me. Just as… just as *you* terrify me."

"Me?" I couldn't wrap my mind around what I was hearing. "How could you be terrified of *me?*"

"Because I barely survived the experience I just described to you. Because if I am wrong about you, as Torqa believes I am – if you turn out to be my enemy, if you shame and ruin me as Elrisa did – I do not feel that I could endure it."

Jesus, no wonder he started off so guarded around me. I'm amazed he's allowed himself to relax around me as quickly as he has, given his history.

"Akzun," I said, coming around the counter and touching his shoulder, "look at me. Please."

He raised his eyes, meeting my gaze with difficulty.

"I understand why you'd feel that way. Why you'd be scared to death of risking so much, of losing everything all over again. Even if you weren't the leader of your people, even if your status as Blood Ruler weren't at stake, it would still be a depressing and frightening prospect. But listen: I'm afraid too, you know? I'm afraid of the dark."

He reacted, confused. "The dark? I do not understand. What do you mean?"

"I mean I have a crippling fear of the dark. I always have, ever since I was a small child. I'd lie in my bed, trembling, crying, paralyzed with fear because I was convinced with every fiber of my being that there were horrible things in the shadows. Things that wanted to hurt me. Sometimes, I even used to wet the bed because I was too terrified to get up and go to the bathroom. I was sure that was the moment that whatever was waiting in the dark would snatch me away forever. And the truth is, I never outgrew those thoughts, those fears. I just waited until I was old enough to have my own place, so I could sleep with the lights on."

"But on Valkred, it is dark almost all of the time."

"Exactly. And yeah, it scares me. A lot. It has ever since you brought me there. Even more so, because on Valkred, there *could* be monsters lurking in the shadows for all I know… watching every move I make, waiting to pounce. But I'm still willing to stay on Valkred to be with you. Because you mean more to me than my fear. Because I care about you, Akzun. Because I'd never betray you – I'd never do what Elrisa did to you. Because I'd do anything to spare you from that. Most of all, because I believe that you will do everything in your power to keep me safe. And I think together, we can help each other face our fears. We can overcome them as long as we believe in each other."

He looked at me for a long moment, then nodded. "I… would like to think that as well. I would like to trust in you, in what we've found with each other. But it is… difficult."

"Of course it is. Trusting your heart to someone when you've been hurt before might be the hardest thing in the world – in the universe – to do. But I'm willing to try if you are."

He took me in his arms, kissing me, holding onto me tightly, as though he were drowning and I was the only thing keeping him afloat. I relaxed against his body, giving in completely, letting him rely on me for comfort. I wanted to be whatever he needed, whatever would help him feel safe.

"It'll be easier once we've had this time to ourselves," I told him. "And when the war is over. When you're not being pulled in a hundred different directions – by Torqa, by the Mana, by your own people. Then we can each focus on being what the other person needs."

"I believe you are right," he whispered in my ear. "Thank you. For reassuring me. For making me feel I can truly believe in someone again. You have given me a great gift, Carly. One I feel I can never fully repay."

"Well, you can start with dinner," I said with a laughed. "Are we eating in here?"

"No, actually. I had something rather more romantic in mind. Please, follow me."

He placed the serving dishes, glasses, utensils, and wine bottle on a hovering tray and led me out of the galley, a mischievous gleam in his eye.

Chapter Eighteen

Akzun

I brought Carly to my private cabin – it was at the front of the ship, just beneath the flight deck.

The placement of the captain's suite was designed to make a very specific statement: that even if a leader chose to cower in his quarters in times of danger instead of remain on the main bridge of the vessel, he'd still be just as much at risk as those under his command.

But there was another, more pleasurable reason for its location at the Wrath's foremost point. One that I was eager to show Carly.

As she stepped in and looked straight ahead of her, her eyes widened. "Oh, Akzun… it's beautiful! Are they some kind of view screens, giving us a live feed from the front of the ship, or…?"

I smiled. This was precisely the reaction I'd hoped for. "No, Carly. They are exactly what they appear to be – windows, standing between us and the endless black ocean of the cosmos."

Three entire walls of the high-ceilinged room were composed of a special, nearly impenetrable substance that was perfectly transparent on one side, but blended flawlessly with the external marble of the ship's armor on the other. The windows were angled in such a way that the stars outside seemed to surround us, flying past us in brilliant streaks and hues as we soared through space at speeds faster than light.

"Does this frighten you?" I asked, placing my hand on her upper arm gently. "Some people have been known to find the effect somewhat unnerving at first."

"I guess I should, right? But for some reason, I don't. I'm just… overwhelmed by it all. I mean, it actually feels like we're zooming through space without a ship! It's spectacular!"

"I hoped you would feel that way," I admitted, "given your fascination with flying. Are you enjoying the wine?"

She took another sip from her glass, raising an eyebrow. "Hard to say. It's very different from what I'm used to. On Earth, the only wine people like me can afford comes in a cardboard box, and tastes like cheap grape juice mixed with antifreeze. Come to think of it, that's probably what it actually is."

"Ah yes, the inequality of your home planet rears its ugly head once more," I said with a sigh.

"Sorry." She shrugged. "I don't mean to be such a downer. I guess it's hard for me to not think about it, given how much luxury I've been surrounded by since…"

"Since I purchased you," I finished for her. "Surely, you must know by now that I no longer think of you as merely my possession?"

Carly tilted her head to one side. "That's a funny way of putting it. You no longer think of me as your possession, or as *merely* your possession?"

"I'm uncertain that I recognize the distinction," I replied uneasily. "But then, as you know, English is not my native tongue. No doubt there are certain subtleties which elude me."

But that wasn't true. I hated having to pretend that it was simply a language issue on my part that prevented me from acknowledging the meaning behind her words. The fact was, it was simply a road I wasn't prepared to go down with her yet – perhaps not ever. I couldn't reconcile my original motivation in acquiring her with my current feelings toward her. Was she my blood slave? My guest? My mate? Surely, she could not be all of them at once.

Earlier, in the galley, I'd detected nothing but honesty in her scent. She had no intention of ever betraying me. She did care for me, truly and deeply. I hadn't been able to detect Elrisa's falsehoods – we were the same race, after all, and she'd trained herself well when it came to hiding her true thoughts and feelings, even when we opened ourselves up to each other telepathically.

Humans had no such defenses against the Valkred. Due to the quirks of their physiology, we could sometimes smell untruths on their skin, in their very blood, no matter how convincingly their mouths lied.

She trusted me. She wanted me. She no longer considered herself my prisoner.

All of these were good things.

But did they mean I could easily let go of the idea that I'd paid for her to be mine? My blood slave, my property, meant to finally quench the horrid thirst that threatened to drive me insane? If I admitted to myself – and to her – that she was free of such obligations to me, what would I do if she chose to exercise her newfound autonomy? What if I needed her blood, needed to make love to her, or both, and she used her freedom to deny me?

What would I do then?

I wasn't sure, and I couldn't bear the uncertainty.

"Come," I said, offering my hand and trying to change the subject, "let me show you something special."

Carly allowed me to lead her to the window, and I pointed out a nearby nebula – churning clouds of red and pink, with a fiercely-glowing white core that was almost too blinding to look at. Ethereal crimson tendrils reached out from it on all sides, curling and swirling and coiling.

"What is that?" she breathed, drinking the last of the wine from her glass and putting it aside on a nearby table.

"One of the natural cosmic phenomena used to denote the borders of the Valkred Empire," I told her. "An extremely rare collection of ignited gas clouds, signifying the heat death of one star and the birth of another from its ashes."

"Like a phoenix," Carly pointed out. "A mythical bird on Earth, which bursts into flame only to be reborn again."

I nodded. "An appropriate comparison. The Mana refer to this nebula as *Gluk'Taag*, 'the great jellyfish.' We Valkred call it the *Kardiiya* – a word that loosely translates to the beating heart of a living creature, and the complex system of blood vessels that extends from it. Funny, isn't it? How each culture gazes up at the stars, and sees something different in them. The shapes we perceive in them – the legends we invent around them – say far more about ourselves than any objective truth the galaxy has to offer. However, when our planets' scientists first reported the recharging of the solar atoms within the anomaly, the renewal of its stellar radiation, M'ruvev and I both saw the same thing: a cataclysmic conclusion to what was old and unnecessary, and the beginning of something new and wonderful."

"The end of the war," she guessed. "The start of a fresh chapter in the relations between your worlds. Maintaining that kind of optimism in front of your people couldn't have been easy, huh?"

I shook my head. "No. It was not."

She put a hand on my shoulder. "It can still happen, Akzun. I believe that with all of my heart. And I'll do everything I can to help you achieve it. But for now, let's eat, huh? Before the emptiness in my stomach causes a black hole to form there, and we have to give that a name, too."

I laughed, gesturing to the meal. "Very well, then. Sit. Eat."

Carly picked up a mollusk with her fork, lifted it to her mouth – then paused, noticing that I wasn't eating anything. She lowered the fork again slowly. "You know, I've never actually seen you eat anything. Unless you count that fake blood stuff. Do you even consume, you know, regular food?"

"From time to time, yes. Mostly to amuse myself with the various flavors, and the means of preparing them. As you've seen, cooking is something of a hobby for me. Many other Valkred rarely bother with it. Some even see it as an affectation, an indulgent pretension exclusively for the wealthy and powerful among us. But it is only the blood that truly sustains members of my race." I tried to keep my voice even, but I was uncomfortable with this line of questioning.

"Uh-huh. And how often do you need to drink… blood?" It looked like she had completely lost interest in the food in front of her.

I sighed. "The artificial plasma must be imbibed almost daily, in order to stave off the cravings. However, in order to remain alive and maintain our good health, real blood must be had every four or five days. Otherwise, we become weak. Our bones grow frail, our flesh thins and blisters, our teeth loosen, the feathers fall from our wings, and we grow more susceptible to the ill effects of sunlight. It is a most unpleasant spectacle, I assure you. One I intend to spare you from witnessing." I paused, then added, "Then again, mated couples can sometimes go a bit longer without feeding."

Carly raised her eyebrows quizzically. "*Mates, mated.* This isn't the first time I've heard you use those terms. Clearly, they have great significance to your people, but how? What do those words mean to you?"

"I'll be happy to show you in the fullness of time," I assured her. "Meanwhile, if you have no desire to eat after all, perhaps I can come up with another way for us to occupy ourselves, hm?"

She smiled. "Why, Blood Ruler, what*ever* could you mean?"

This, I thought at her, folding my arms – and my wings – around her tightly and kissing her.

She returned the embrace eagerly, opening her thoughts to me once more. This time, though, I didn't rush to join our minds and hearts. I was more careful, more guarded, my essence hovering just outside the edge of her consciousness as if I were lurking in the doorway to her soul.

You can come in, her mind whispered to me as her tongue playfully flicked against the tip of mine. ***I like swimming in your thoughts. It's refreshing, like slipping into a cool pond on a hot summer day.***

No, I replied, raking my nails gently against the nape of her neck. By the stars, the taste of her warm breath was making my heart race. Her jugular was so tantalizingly close… ***I do not wish to overwhelm or confuse you.***

I can take it, Akzun. I promise. And hey… maybe I want to be "overwhelmed."

I resisted, pulling away with my mind even as I held her closer to my body, but surprisingly, her thoughts followed mine insistently, pursuing them, cornering them like a Frenzien Gorehound chasing its prey up a tree.

I'd never encountered a human with such a forceful mind, and I was taken aback by it. Even most Valkred couldn't push into my thoughts unless I granted them access. Clearly, Carly was a very special woman – more special than even I had realized until now.

I caressed her upper arms tenderly, feeling goose bumps rise there, seeing the fine hairs on the back of her neck stand up. And just inches away, major arteries, throbbing with blood, red rivers gushing and flowing, ready for me to bury my face in them and lap them up…

I had to distract myself. If I couldn't claim her blood, I needed to console myself with her body.

But you can ***claim my blood.***

The thought appeared in my mind so sharply and suddenly that I physically recoiled with surprise, staring at her. Her eyes met mine unflinchingly, her head cocked to one side in a silent challenge.

"Yes, you heard me right," she said with a grin. "You want to bite me? You want to taste my blood? You can. I don't mind. Really."

How could I possibly respond to that? How could I fully communicate my reasons for holding back without frightening her – without making her want to run from me, screaming, finally convinced that I am truly the vampire that haunts the legends of her world? Right now, she saw me as a lover, not a danger, not a predator.

I didn't want to change that. I couldn't, no matter the cost.

Instead, I slammed the doors to my mind as hard as I could and focused entirely on the physical, hoping Carly would simply be caught up in the moment with me and forget all thoughts of blood. I picked her up and carried her to the weightless, undulating gel-form mattress in the corner of the room.

As I lowered her onto it, she let out a soft gasp.

"My God – Akzun, it's amazing! I've never felt anything like this."

I grinned, desperately trying to banish my hunger. "It is meant to simulate utter weightlessness, even in an environment with artificial gravity. It's designed to provide a restful slumber, but in certain other circumstances, the effects can be most… stimulating."

"Mmm, show me," she murmured, wriggling a bit to slip out of her clothes and drop them on the floor.

I undid my tunic and trousers, casting them aside and flexing my wings. I enjoyed the awed expression on her face as she took in my full wingspan; I imagined that to her, I must have resembled one of the fierce and mighty angels from her Earth mythology, a divine engine of beauty and destruction.

I placed my hands on her knees, spreading them apart. I could see that she was already wet, her labia glistening, her reddish-blonde hairs beaded with dewdrops of lust. There was a blush high on her cheeks, and she was breathing hard, waiting for me to take her.

I slid onto the bed and leaned forward, delicately pressing the tip of my thumb against her clit. She twitched and moaned, and I began to move my thumb in a slow circle, teasing her, relishing her moisture against my skin. Her pungent musk filled my nostrils, briefly eclipsing the scent of her blood.

I pushed my thumb inside her, angling it upward to press against the spongy, sticky wall. She hissed my name urgently, both out loud and inside my head – my mind was still tightly shut, yet she was able to make herself heard there anyway.

Fascinating. Intriguing. And *so* alluring.

Unable to wait any longer, I withdrew my hand and positioned myself between her legs. She wrapped them around me immediately, hugging my sides tightly between her thighs. My cock was hard, throbbing against the lips of her pussy – and then, with a single push, I was inside her.

"Oh Akzun," she begged, "please, give me everything you've got… take me, make me yours… "

Our hips thrust against each other so hard the impact almost hurt, yet we still quickened our pace steadily, hungrily, our sweating bodies sliding together marvelously. Her nails dug into my back, and she arched her neck, closing her eyes and exposing her throat to me.

"Drink from me," Carly drawled deliciously.

"No," I panted. I plunged myself inside her even harder, hoping I could distract her. "I cannot do that."

"You can," she insisted, opening her eyes again and taking my face in her hands. "It's all right. I want you to. Look inside my mind, and you'll see."

I seized her wrists suddenly, pinning her to the bed and slamming myself into her with all my might. She cried out sharply, mouth falling open in silent gasps, but her eyes never left mine. The bloodlust was rising in me, surging, tidal in its ferocity. I had to maintain control, but by the stars, it was almost too much for me to bear.

"You do not know what you ask of me," I snarled, carefully annunciating each word. "I cannot feed on you. Ever. You do not know what will happen if I do."

Carly shook her head. "Whatever it is, I'm not afraid. I want to feed you, to nourish you when you need it. If the blood slaves in the lower levels of the castle can survive it, I can, too. I know you won't hurt me."

I couldn't take it anymore. If I didn't pull away from her – if I didn't leave the room at once – I would no longer be able to resist the bloodlust. I would feed, and feed, and feed, until…

Carly was looking up at me with a strange mixture of curiosity and pity. "But *you're* afraid, aren't you?"

I reared back, dislodging myself from her and grabbing my clothes from the floor.

"You are merely a human," I sneered, getting dressed quickly. "You know nothing of the galaxy outside your own planet, of the Valkred, or of me. Perhaps it would be wiser for you to be frightened of me, after all."

As I stormed out of the room, she called out after me, choking back tears. "Yeah? And maybe you shouldn't have paid two hundred and fifty thousand whatever-the-fucks on a meal you *aren't even going to eat,* asshole!"

The truth of her words stung, and I allowed the door to close behind me, rubbing my temples with my eyes closed.

I wasn't strong enough for this.

So how in the names of all the Succubi could I possibly be strong enough to lead an empire?

Chapter Nineteen

Carly

As soon as Akzun left, I rolled over onto my side, sobbing, and feeling like my emotions were pulling me in a hundred directions at once.

Why wouldn't he drink my blood? Why was he trying to distance himself from me again? Why was there suddenly so much tension between us, when he'd seemed so relaxed and open before?

And more than that: Why the fuck did I *care* so much?

He was an *alien vampire*, for Christ's sake. And worse, he'd bought me from some scummy bartender like I was livestock. He showed no remorse about putting more money into an intergalactic slave trade that had led to the abduction and abuse of countless people from Earth. People like me, who were routinely terrorized, treated like shit – even sexually assaulted, if what Miranda had told me about the collars was true.

So why did I want so badly to be with him, to stay in his castle on Valkred and give him whatever he needed from me… even if what he needed was my blood?

Because even through all the bullshit, I could sense the good in him. More than that, some part of me saw the potential for *greatness* in him, the chance for him to change things in the galaxy for the better. With the support of someone who truly cared about him – someone who *believed* in him – I was convinced that he could do amazing things. He could end the war with the Mana, and save the lives of his people. He could be a kind and benevolent ruler. He could enact policies that would ensure the blood slaves were treated better, and perhaps even end the practice of slavery altogether eventually.

Maybe he could even use his diplomatic influence to correct the imbalance of wealth and power on Earth. He clearly felt strongly about the injustice that existed there.

If he had the right woman behind him, there was no limit to what he might accomplish.

There was all of that. But there was something else, too – something that was harder to admit, a magnetism between us that couldn't be denied.

As crazy as it made me feel – as insane as anyone on Earth would think I was – I knew that I was in love with him. I'd never met any man like him on my own world, and I was sure I never would. It felt like I'd been waiting for Akzun my entire life, and now that I had him, I didn't want to let him go.

Was that such a ludicrous concept? That I could find the love of my life in the arms of an extraterrestrial warrior-king with wings and fangs?

Yeah. It was. But it didn't change the fact that it was true.

So what was I supposed to do about it?

As if on cue, the doors to the captain's quarters slid open and Akzun strode in. He was obviously trying to maintain a neutral expression, but he still seemed vaguely embarrassed. "I… have something to show you," he said, clearing his throat.

"Yeah?" I wiped the tears from my cheeks, sniffling. I hated giving him the satisfaction of seeing me cry, but there wasn't much I could do about it now. "What's that?"

He gestured at the main panel of the window – the one whose angle matched the very front of the ship. I turned to look, and my breath froze in my chest.

A tiny blue marble hung in space, shrouded in clouds, surrounded by the specks of orbiting satellites.

Earth.

"I have brought you home," he said. "You are free."

I stood up, walking over to the glass slowly. The sight was bizarre, not to mention beautiful. I knew seeing Earth like this should have made me homesick, eager to bridge the distance from the ship to the planet and set foot on familiar soil. From this distance, it was hard to imagine all of the poverty and greed and strife that covered the surface of my home world like a blight.

But those things were there. I had seen them firsthand – God, I had seen too much of them. And I knew that they were still there, waiting for me.

It made me sad. And scared. And angry.

"You… want to get rid of me?" I whispered incredulously, hot tears spilling down my face again. "You don't want me around anymore, so you're just going to throw me away?"

Akzun looked genuinely confused. "No! That was not my intention at all!"

"Oh? Then what are your *intentions*, huh? 'Cause I've got to tell you, I'm getting pretty tired of trying to guess."

"After our last… interaction… I assumed you no longer wished to remain with me," Akzun said uncomfortably. "I believed you would want to go back to your own world. I'm giving you a chance to return to your previous life."

I sighed. "No, Akzun, I told you: I didn't have much of a life on Earth. What I really want is to build a new life with you. But I can't do that if you won't talk to me. – if you refuse to tell me what you're so scared of, why you're so intent on keeping your distance from me. It can't just be because of what happened with Elrisa. You can't possibly still mistrust me that much."

He shook his head sadly. "It's not that, Carly. I do trust you. I believe you when you say that you care about me, that you would never betray me the way she did. That's the problem. I… care about you, as well. Too much to risk harming you."

"So you're telling me there's really no way for you to drink from me without… what? Hurting me, or something? I mean, if it's just pain we're talking about, hey, I can take it. I could probably get used to it.

Hell, maybe I could even learn to like it, in a weird way. Humans are like that, you know?"

"There are ways for my race to feed without causing any serious injury, yes, under normal circumstances. But this is different. I am in the grip of a condition that occurs in all Valkred at a certain stage of our lives. A bloodlust. It makes feeding… dangerous. Once I begin drinking from you, there is a very real possibility that I could lose control and end up damaging you irrevocably, or killing you."

"Then why did you buy me?" I asked, confused. "It doesn't make any sense."

"You are correct – it does not. When I first purchased you from Nos, I believed my actions were based on a superficial need to feed. But the more time I spent with you, the more I realized that this was not my true intention after all. It never was. I claimed you for my own because I could not bear the idea of anyone else having you. Because… I want you for my mate."

"But earlier, you said mates could feed from each other," I pointed out. "You said it made the cravings easier to control."

"Again, under normal circumstances, yes. However, my bloodlust means that in this case, we cannot proceed in such a way."

"Isn't there any cure for this bloodlust? Doesn't it go away eventually?"

Akzun hung his head. "It is difficult to say. The outcome differs among members of my race. For now, though, it seems to show no signs of abating."

I crossed the distance between us, holding his face in my hands and bringing his eyes up to meet mine. He resisted for a moment, then relented.

"I might not know much about the Valkred," I said, "but I know that there must be some way for us to move past this. And I know we'll find that path together. What we have is too important to give up on. And until we figure out how to beat this, I'm not leaving you – I'll do anything it takes to help you feel better."

I leaned forward, kissing him and stroking the sides of his head tenderly. I felt him pull back for the briefest of moments – felt the hesitation in his thoughts, the fear, even though I was relatively certain he was trying to guard his mind against mine.

Then, suddenly, it was as though a dam inside of him broke, and everything within him spilled out into me – his desire, his need to connect with me, to trust me.

To be with me. To make me his, no matter the cost.

I planted a series of soft kisses down his neck and chest, slowly lowering myself to my knees in front of him. It was sexual, yes, but it was more than that, too. I wanted to make him tower over me, to make him feel powerful. I wanted to make him believe that whatever happened, he would be fully in control. I wanted to make him feel like he was a worthy leader, and a worthy mate.

His cold fingers ran through my hair, stroking my temples, encouraging me. I undid his trousers, releasing his cock from its confinement – it was already stiff for me, reaching out, searching for the comfort only I could provide. I took it in my hands, running my palms up and down the shaft.

Akzun let out a lustful sigh, and when I looked up, I could see that his eyes were closed, his head tilted upward, allowing himself to fully bask in this moment, this sensation.

Good.

I breathed gently on his cock, teasing him. He looked down, surprised, and I gave him a mischievous grin, coaxing a smile from him.

You take yourself way too seriously sometimes, Akzun, I thought, hoping he'd hear me.

Then I took the tip of him in my mouth, sucking him lightly as my fingertips kneaded the base of his shaft. He inhaled sharply and resumed caressing my hair. The tip of my tongue flicked against the sensitive spot just under the tip and he let out a long, low, appreciative moan. I waited until I was sure he couldn't take it anymore, then moved my head forward, taking his entire length all the way to the back of my throat.

I felt a shudder travel up the length of his spine. *Oh, my precious Carly. No one has ever made me feel the way you do.*

Then you'd better get ready, Blood Ruler, 'cause I'm just getting started.

I let my tongue travel up and down the underside of his cock, feeling it throb against the roof of my mouth. His hands tightened on the back of my head, grabbing fiercely at locks of my hair. Just when it felt like he might lose control, I pulled back, sliding out of my pants and spreading my legs wide for him. I was wetter than I'd ever been in my life, and I couldn't wait to have him inside me.

I'm all yours, Akzun. Take me. Show me what it means to be your mate.

Akzun lunged on top of me – no hesitation this time, no holding back, an unstoppable force of pure desire. He slid between my legs like a champion diver slipping into a pool, and as he penetrated me, I embraced him, screaming his name with my voice and my mind.

I tightened the lips of my pussy around his shaft – feeling him move in and out as I ran my fingers over his wide, muscular back. He plunged into me so deeply and passionately that the room started to spin around me, and for a moment, I thought I might faint from the pure sensory overload of his lovemaking… his voice echoing in my head, his feelings pushing into my heart, the jagged words and phrases overlapping like the shattered shards of some perfectly beautiful stained glass window.

His mate. I was his mate. He'd never wanted anyone so desperately before, and he knew he never would again. He had to have me forever. He wanted my body, my soul. He craved my blood, fevered for it, but he could never hurt me, never, never, never, not for anything in the galaxy… he…

(… Loved? Was that a concept he knew, something he understood, something he was capable of?)

He needed me.

I was his strength, his heart, everything he'd spent his life looking for. I was more important to him than anything – Elrisa, the respect of his people, his status as Blood Ruler.

He surged and pulsed within me, his cock finding places inside me that no one had ever reached before. I was aching, spasms of pleasure and pain twanging the muscles of my inner thighs like guitar strings, and I was breathing so hard I thought I might hyperventilate.

I felt his climax rain down on my core like a sudden, deliciously cold monsoon. My own orgasm followed swiftly, pouring through me, pure ecstasy drenching and saturating every cell in my body. My hips bucked and twitched against his, and we held each other so tightly that it felt like we might merge into a single being of pure joy.

What shall we do now, my darling one? he asked, his thoughts tinged with blissful peace.

I smiled. "Let's head back home, Blood Ruler. Your people need you."

Chapter Twenty

Akzun

As the Angel's Wrath approached Valkred, I tapped the keys on the communications console, then frowned.

"Is something wrong?" Carly asked.

"I'm not sure. I'm trying to reach Zark so he can give me a report of anything that might have happened while we were gone. We should be within comm range...in fact, we should have been able to reach him as soon as we re-entered the borders of our empire. But for some reason, I can't seem to get through to him, or any of our planetary defense outposts. There's something interfering with the ship's comm array."

"Is it a problem?"

I shrugged. "It's a bit curious, that's all. The comms were in perfect working order when we left. But no matter. The defense platforms will analyze the ship's data to determine our identities, and I can have Lun repair the communication system when we return to the Ruby Stronghold."

She nodded, settling back in her chair.

Sure enough, our trip back to Valkred went smoothly, despite the communications blackout. The defense platforms automatically disarmed to allow us safe passage, the Wrath descended through Valkred's dense purple atmosphere, and we touched down lightly on the castle's docking pad. It was morning on this part of the planet's surface, and the pale pinkish rays of sunlight made me shield my photosensitive eyes until I had a chance to let them adjust.

As we walked down the ramp and onto the tarmac, we were greeted by a contingent of bodyguards, led by Zark. He looked anxious.

"Thank the Succubi you're back!" Zark breathed. "We've been trying to reach you for over an hour! Why didn't you answer?"

"There's something wrong with the ship's comm system," I replied, apprehension beginning to replace the peace I'd cultivated with Carly. "Why? What's going on?"

"Our military intelligence services received numerous reports indicating that a group of Mana saboteurs are here on Valkred."

"What? How the hell did they make it past our sentry posts?" I demanded.

"We don't know. But they've been spotted in the Tor'Ador Sector. And there's only one high-value target in that area…"

"The gem mines. One of our planet's main trade resources. If they succeed in disabling or destroying them, they could financially cripple Valkred for years, perhaps even decades. Damn them." My hands curled into fists at my side. "Have you contacted M'ruvev?"

"Yes. He's on his way, and our defense forces have been ordered to let him through so he can help us deal with this."

"If we take the Wrath, or any other vessels, they'll see us coming and scatter," I mused aloud. "We probably won't have another chance to round them up. And we need them alive, Zark. We need them to tell us who's been behind all of this."

"What are you going to do, Akzun?" Carly asked.

I unfurled my wings, and Zark did likewise. "We'll have to fly there. Carly, you go up to your chamber and wait for me there." I turned to the guards. "You're coming with us. Let's go find these cowards and end their campaign of violence and treachery once and for all!"

The guards cheered, raising their laser-staves and extending their wings. I saw the nervous look on Carly's face and kissed her, no longer caring who else witnessed our true feelings for each other. "Don't fret, my dear. I'll deal with these Mana swiftly and return soon."

"Just be careful," she pleaded.

"I will. I promise."

I took off from the tarmac, Zark and the others following me in close formation. Inwardly, I wished I'd had time to adorn myself with armor and more formidable weaponry, but at least I had my blaster clipped to my side – it would have to do.

We soared high above the capitol city and beyond, the people busily teeming far below us like colonies of Korvaat Labor-Ants. Soon, the gem mines came into view on the horizon.

"Fan out around the entrance to the mines," I ordered the guards. "Search the area thoroughly. They'll probably have remote-detonator explosives rigged to create a cave-in and entomb the workers inside. Zark, you're with me."

The guards nodded, veering off. Zark and I surveyed the flat grey plains surrounding the mine.

"Look, brother!" Zark exclaimed after a few moments, pointing at a sloping grassy area.

I followed his gaze, squinting. "I don't see anything."

"Exactly. So what's casting those shadows on the ground?"

Then I saw it – a cluster of murky shadows, vaguely humanoid-shaped. My eyes widened with understanding. "By the stars. They're using personalized cloaks."

Zark nodded. "We knew they'd been trying to develop cloaking technology. We assumed it was for their vessels, but what if it was for their troops instead? It'd take far less energy to build and power such devices." He spoke into his communicator. "All units, converge on our location. We've found them.

They're cloaked. Proceed with extreme caution – we don't know whether they've armed the explosives yet."

"Understood, sir," the lead guard replied.

Zark and I touched down on the plain, aiming our weapons at the area where the shadows were standing.

"We know you're there, and we know what you're planning to do," I announced loudly. "Disengage your cloaking devices and surrender at once."

No answer. I may as well have been talking to thin air.

"Very well," Zark smirked. "The hard way, then." He fired his laser-staff, and the air shimmered and crackled where the bolt connected with its target. There was a plume of smoke that seemed to drift up from nowhere, and a yowl of agony.

Then, one by one, the cloaking devices disengaged – revealing half a dozen figures in modified Mana battle suits and helmets, armed with trident-shaped blasters.

They took up offensive positions and returned fire.

There was nowhere for us to take cover, and the hail of lasers pelted us. I took a hit to the left shoulder immediately, followed by another hit to the right hip. The pain was sharp, but I fought through it, focusing on my aim as I squeezed the trigger of my own blaster.

I hit one of the attackers in the head and he went down, his face reduced to a smoldering crater. Another pair of shots from my blaster cut the legs out from under a second one.

A blast grazed the side of Zark's head, charring his long purple hair. He let out a shriek of rage and fired wildly, managing to catch a third enemy square in the chest.

Three to go. We needed to take them alive, but how could we in the face of such a barrage?

A fourth saboteur charged straight for me, ignoring several blasts to his torso and arms until he was close enough to raise his gun right in my face. There was no way I could survive a shot at point blank range, and for a chilling second I thought it was all over for me.

Then a bolt from above incinerated him, and the rest of our guards swooped in, swiftly knocking the tridents from the attackers' gauntlets and bringing them to the ground in a single coordinated strike. The saboteurs were hopelessly outnumbered.

"Blood Ruler!" one of the guards exclaimed. "You've been hurt!"

"I'll be fine," I hissed through clenched teeth. The pain was almost unbearable, but I couldn't afford to let it show. "Contact our orbital defense forces and find out whether M'ruvev has arrived yet."

"We just received word that he has, sir."

"Good. Have his ship routed to these coordinates," I ordered. "Let him see what his own people tried to do, and let's clear this up once and for all."

"That… might be a bit easier said than done, brother," Zark said uneasily, pulling the helmet from one of the attackers. "Look."

I peered at the face of the would-be saboteur, and my jaw dropped.

He was a Valkred.

"What is the meaning of this?" I growled, marching over to him and putting my boot on his throat. "Why are you wearing these Mana uniforms? Why were you attempting to destroy the gem mines?"

"Because our people deserve to know what a threat the Mana are, and how foolish their Blood Ruler is for ignoring that!" he gurgled, his fangs bared. "That is why we plotted the destruction of the Aquavor, and the dismantling of the gem mines! We needed the Valkred to reject this inane treaty before it's too late, and the real Mana come to take everything from us!"

"Are any others working with you?" Zark asked quietly.

"No, but it doesn't matter," he wheezed. "There were only seven of us, and look at all we've managed to accomplish! So go ahead, take us into custody. Let the others of our race see what true courage and determination looks like. Let them hear our motivations, and the righteousness of our cause… then watch as our seven becomes seven hundred, then seven thousand. Our movement will spread across the empire, and we will see you ousted as Blood Ruler at last! Replaced with someone who truly has our best interests at heart – someone with strength, with the will to fight this war and win it. *Someone who doesn't waste his time flirting with some human blood slave!*"

I looked down at his face, saw the fanatical devotion burning in his crimson eyes, just as a shadow fell over us all. A Mana shuttle was hovering overhead. It touched down softly, and the hatch opened, revealing M'ruvev and a pair of armed Mana guards.

M'ruvev peered at the Valkred in Mana battle suits, and his wet, glassy eyes twitched. "What in the name of all the oceans is going on here, Akzun?"

"We've found the terrorists responsible for attacking the Aquavor, M'ruvev. We caught them trying to blow up our gem mines. Their goal was to sow fear and mistrust between our people, in order to prolong the war."

"I see." M'ruvev nodded pensively. "I am deeply relieved to hear that you've managed to resolve this, old friend. Now, I feel it would be appropriate for us to take them into custody, so they can face justice for their crimes against our world."

"We're eager to cooperate with you," I told him, "but letting you take them alive might pose a bit of a problem."

"Oh? How so?"

"We're concerned that others who hear their testimony might be sympathetic to their cause," Zark explained. "They could spawn imitators – not just on Valkred, but on your planet as well."

"Then what do you propose?" M'ruvev asked.

"We could end this right here," I suggested. "We could kill them, and claim that they left us no other option. Then we could jointly announce that the treaty has been restored, without anyone asking too many questions about the negotiations that led us to such a conclusion. It's not a perfect solution, but to me, it seems like the best course of action."

M'ruvev nodded again. "That outcome would be acceptable. I can only hope that no one else gets the same idea these Valkred had and attempts to threaten the peace again."

"They might," I conceded. "For that matter, your people might, as well. But you and I can take this opportunity, here and now, to continue to enforce the treaty no matter what. To trust in each other, and to work together from this point forward in rooting out such conspiracies among our own."

"I am willing to commit to that," M'ruvev agreed. "However, I do have one final request: that I dispense this justice upon the remaining traitors myself."

"Certainly," I said.

M'ruvev stood over the attackers as one of his guards handed him a trident-pistol. "I had many friends aboard the Aquavor the day it was destroyed," he murmured, his voice tinged with sadness and anger. "What I do now, I do in their names."

"*Damn* you, Akzun!" the traitor roared, struggling to free himself from the grip of my guards. "*You* are the true betrayer of Valkred, for allowing these fish-faced scum to murder your own people while you stand and watch! This is not over, do you hear me? You cannot silence us, you cannot defeat us! More like us will rise up to defend our world against your cowardice and weakness, I swear to you –"

His words were sharply cut off by the single shot from M'ruvev's blaster, followed by two more – one for each of the remaining saboteurs. The shots echoed off the grass.

"And now you have your revenge," I said to M'ruvev. "I hope it was satisfying."

"No," he whispered mournfully, returning the blaster to his guard. "But I suppose it will have to do."

Chapter Twenty-One

Carly

I sat on the bed in my chamber, worrying about Akzun – hoping he was able to survive and triumph over whatever threats were waiting for him at the gem mines.

No, that wasn't true. Or at least, it wasn't the *whole* truth.

The whole truth was, I was still tied up in knots about our relationship. It was clear that he wanted to be with me, but how could we ever truly relax as long as his bloodlust was standing in the way of our happiness? He could call me his mate all he liked, but I'd seen the truth in his thoughts: On this world, *real* mates fed from each other. It was natural, expected, even required. Without that dynamic, it would be like an Earth couple trying to make a relationship work without sex.

In a word? Frustrating.

I heard footsteps in the corridor, and for a moment, I thought Akzun had returned – but no, the steps were too light to be his, or even Dhako's or Zark's. I hopped up and went to the door, thinking it might be a messenger with news about Akzun.

Just as I got to the door, a hooded figure appeared in it, holding a curved silver dagger – and swinging right at my face.

I ducked reflexively, and the blade missed me, nicking the marble door frame.

"What the fuck!" I exclaimed.

The voice that answered was muffled by the heavy cowl that hid the attacker's face, but was still unmistakable.

"You've taken advantage of our hospitality long enough, you feeble human whore," Torqa said nastily, bringing the knife back for another strike.

I dodged under the next swing, pushing past her into the hallway. Based on the way Torqa had treated me before, I shouldn't have been surprised by her sudden assault, but I guess I'd assumed she'd be too scared of Akzun's wrath to actually make a move on me.

Big mistake. Huge.

I was desperate to get to the stairs, to call for help – but Torqa overtook me immediately, hooking her boot around my ankle to trip me. I fell on my face and flipped over, scrambling backward as she advanced menacingly.

"How could you possibly believe you'd be a suitable mate for our Blood Ruler?" Torqa snarled, raising the knife over her head. "How could a mewling, squirming piece of Earthling trash like you ever do anything but weaken him and shame our planet?"

The blade came down, and I rolled to the side just in time to avoid it. The stairs were closer. Maybe I could find one of the palace guards on the lower levels… but would they help me? Or would they be loyal to Torqa? How could I be sure?

"You are less than nothing!" Torqa slashed at me again, narrowly missing my jugular. "You are merely a symptom of Akzun's doubt and uncertainty regarding the idiotic treaty with the Mana. He wants to believe in romantic notions of peace and unity in the galaxy, when in reality, there is only *strength and conquest!* He needs a mate who will make him hard as iron, not soften him with fairy tales. *He needs me!*"

I barely made it to my feet before dodging another strike from Torqa. *Christ*, she was fast. Strong, too – based on the marks her dagger was making in the marble walls and floors, there was enough power behind her thrusts to carve me in half.

"Could a human woman have manipulated those terrorists into attacking the Aquavor?" Torqa swung the blade at my face, and I darted backward just in time for it to graze the tip of my nose. "Could some worthless blood slave bought in a filthy, backwater bar have convinced them to try to blow up the gem mines, *all while making them think it was their idea?* No! That required cunning and a strength of will you will never possess. You may have survived my falling statue, you wretched girl, *but by the stars, you won't survive this!*"

I ducked another knife strike, but Torqa faked me out, making me lean right into her other hand. She gave my chest a solid push and I stumbled backward, feeling the top of the stairs beneath my feet.

I fell, the floor and ceiling spinning and switching places as my head, body, and limbs smacked against the slabs of smooth marble.

Then I heard a man scream my name (*Akzun? Is that you?*), and everything went black.

Chapter Twenty-Two

Akzun

My injuries had been treated by the medics at the mines, and I entered the Ruby Stronghold with Zark at my side, heading for the shaft that led to the upper levels. I was so eager to fly up to Carly, to let her know that I had succeeded in rooting out and defeating the traitors – that I had eliminated the danger to my people and preserved the treaty with the Mana. I was proud, I was happy, I was ready to share my victory with her and take her in my arms again…

Then I heard the noise of a struggle coming from the staircase.

Zark and I exchanged worried looks and ran in that direction. I stormed up the steps with Zark right behind me… then stopped short as Carly tumbled down, her body limp and bloody.

"Carly!" I screamed.

I heard her voice in my head, weakly: ***Akzun? Is that you?***

Then her thoughts went horribly blank.

"Zark, summon Khim! *Now!* Then find out if anyone saw who did this to her!" As Zark ran off, I kneeled beside Carly, examining her wounds. There was a gash on her forehead, and blood was pouring down her face. One of her arms was bent at an awful angle, and when she breathed, I could hear several broken ribs grinding together.

But she was alive. Thank the Succubi, she was alive. I could still hear her heartbeat.

As I carried her to my chamber, a strange thought occurred to me: She was bleeding right in my arms. My bloodlust should have overcome me, driving me to drink from her despite my concern for her well-being.

So why wasn't it?

I shook my head, trying to clear it. These were questions for later. For now, I had to make sure she would live through this.

Khim rushed in. "I'm here, Blood Ruler."

"Can you help her?" I pleaded.

She examined Carly briefly, then nodded. "I believe so, yes. But it will require tremendous concentration. I must ask you to leave while I tend to her." Her previous sarcasm about treating a human blood slave was gone, replaced with grim urgency.

"Very well."

As I left the room, Zark approached me, shaking his head. "The guards didn't see anyone enter or leave during the time of the attack, brother. No unfamiliar scents linger, either. It's as though her assailant simply appeared out of thin air, and then vanished."

"*Is this the level of security my guards deem acceptable for the palace of their Blood Ruler?*" I thundered, punching the wall. "*I may as well have no guards at all, for all the good they do! First Torqa waltzes in whenever she pleases, then you, and now this thrice-damned assassin!*"

"I know you're upset, Akzun," Zark said gently, "but you must control yourself. Khim will heal Carly, and we will find out who was responsible for this violation. I promise."

I threw my back against the wall and sank down into a crouch miserably, my head in my hands. "When does it end, Zark? The war, Elrisa, the terrorists… and now this. Can't I enjoy even a moment of peace?"

Zark sat next to me, putting his arm around my shoulder. "Brother, if it's peace you seek, I regret to inform you that you may have chosen the wrong profession."

I laughed weakly. "You may be right. Is it too late for me to become a leech farmer, perhaps?"

"Probably," he chuckled. "Which is a terrible shame, because in my opinion, you would look quite fetching in hip boots."

The door to my chamber opened and Khim emerged, her robes stained with blood. "Zark, would you give us a moment, please?"

Zark left, and I turned to Khim. "Well? Is she healed?"

"Not quite, Blood Ruler. Tell me, please: What is the precise nature of your relationship with this woman? I had initially believed her to be a blood slave you'd purchased during the treaty negotiations, but there are those in the palace who say she might mean considerably more to you than that."

"What possible difference could that make, Khim?" I yelled, grabbing her by the shoulders. "*Can you heal her, or not?*"

"I'm afraid it makes a great deal of difference," Khim replied evenly, her gaze meeting mine unwaveringly. "The woman is carrying a child. One that is part Valkred. I can only assume that it's yours. Am I correct?"

I released her from my grip, my head spinning. "Yes," I said, my voice barely above a whisper. "I suppose it must be."

"Then the remaining course of action depends on your relationship to her," Khim went on patiently, straightening her robes. "She sustained numerous internal injuries during the fall. They threaten her life, and he one within her. If she is merely a blood slave – and therefore, replaceable in your eyes – I would advise that you allow me to ease and expedite her passing. If, on the other hand, you consider her to be a mate, then it seems as though the best course of action is for you to form a blood bond with her. Taking your essence into herself will strengthen both her and the child, allowing them to heal."

"And you're sure this will work?" I demanded.

She shook her head. "No. But it's the best chance she has. And from the expression on your face, Blood Ruler, I believe I can guess your decision. I'll leave you to it, then." She gestured toward the entrance to my chamber, then left.

I entered and stood over her unconscious form. She seemed so small, so vulnerable.

And the life she was carrying inside her was my own offspring.

I'd never seriously contemplated fatherhood before – certainly not with a human woman as the mother – but now that it was staring me in the face, I couldn't bear the thought of losing a child in such a way.

Very well, then, my love, I thought at her. ***If a blood bond is the best chance for you to come back to me, then a blood bond it shall be.***

I waited to see if her mind would respond, but no. Only silence.

I climbed into the bed next to her and gently took her by the wrist, lifting it to my lips. Once again, I was mildly perplexed at my own self-control – I should have been ravenous, foaming at the mouth for her blood, but instead the bloodlust seemed like a distant memory. In that moment, all I cared about was doing whatever it took to preserve her life, and that of our baby.

I took a deep breath and sank my teeth into her skin, feeling the hot blood spurt against the roof of my mouth.

Her taste was sweeter than anything I'd ever known.

I took several deep swallows, feeling her essence flow from her veins into my own like a torrent of pure melted gold. I realized it had been days since I'd fed on real blood, and newfound strength traveled through my muscles and bones. I was renewed, reborn.

My bloodlust was gone – I could clearly see that now – replaced by my love for her. If only I'd been able to see this truth sooner…

I removed my fangs from her flesh, using the bed sheets to staunch the flow of blood. The saliva of the Valkred contained natural coagulants, allowing those we drink from to stop bleeding and heal from our bites quickly.

But that was only half the process. The other half might prove more tricky.

I drew my fangs across my own wrist, opening it. Blood welled up immediately, and I pressed the wound to Carly's lips – hoping enough would trickle down her throat to forge the blood bond as strongly as was required for her and our baby to heal. I kept it there as long as I could, watching the fluid stain her mouth a vivid shade of red.

When I felt I couldn't afford to part with any more blood, I withdrew my wrist and curled up next to her, praying to all the Succubi that it would be enough.

Chapter Twenty-Three

Carly

I woke up with a start, my mind still tumbling down the hard marble steps. I sank my fingernails into the bedspread, waiting for the lurching sensation to stop. After a few seconds, the world went right side up again, and I realized I was in Akzun's bedchamber.

He was sitting in bed next to me, smiling gently. "How are you feeling?"

How was I feeling? I'd been shoved down a flight of stone stairs. I'd felt my ribs splinter, my arm snap, and my skull crack on the final impact.

But for some reason, I felt better than I ever had in my life.

I looked down at my body. Everything seemed to be in place. No cuts, scrapes, fractures, or even bruises. And I was filled with a strange, manic energy. The air tasted sharper on my lips. The scents that flowed into my nostrils with each breath seemed more pronounced and nuanced. Even the colors of everything around me were more vivid and layered somehow. I felt like I could jump up and run five miles. I felt like I could fly!

"Pretty damn good, oddly enough, thanks for asking," I replied. "What happened to me? One minute I was falling, and then…"

"You must be extremely confused right now," Akzun said in a soothing voice, putting his arms around me. "And I will explain everything to your satisfaction, I promise you. But first, there is something I must make you understand."

"Okay, go ahead," I said warily.

"Many of my race go entire lifetimes without ever finding the mate they were destined for," Akzun began. It sounded like he was choosing his words extremely carefully. "But I have been most fortunate. Because I have found you, and you, Carly… you have chosen to return my affections, despite the way things began for us, despite all the universe has done to test our feelings for each other."

"Well, that's a very sweet 'Get Well Soon' card you've come up with," I joked, "but I'm still not sure I understand what happened, or why I feel this way. I'm so filled with… with… "

"Energy?" he suggested with a grin. "Life? Yes, I suppose things would feel quite different for you now. You are experiencing the world as we Valkred do. Your senses are heightened. You perceive the world differently. You have new strength, speed, and stamina. You feel as though you can do things now that you would never have dreamed of before."

"Yeah, right, but *why?*" I demanded. "What aren't you telling me, Akzun?"

"Your wounds were quite severe, Carly," he said. "Khim told me that I would have to form a blood bond with you in order to save your life. In order to save… *both* of your lives."

He placed a hand on my belly meaningfully, and I gasped. "You mean…?"

Akzun nodded. "Yes. You are carrying my child. And now, you are carrying my blood as well. Just as… just as I am carrying yours."

"I… wow, Jesus, I don't know what to say," I breathed, my heart thumping in my throat. "I guess I just assumed there was no way I could get pregnant with a, you know…"

"Alien?" he filled in.

"Yeah. With an alien. And now you're telling me – I mean, is Khim *sure* about this?"

"Yes."

"And you…" I swallowed hard, trying to process all this new information. "You drank my blood? I thought you said the bloodlust meant you couldn't… that *we* couldn't…"

"I apologize, Carly. I am uncertain of how this has happened. I'd been in the grip of the bloodlust ever since I was forced to have Elrisa executed. I was beginning to think I'd never be rid of it. But now, somehow, it seems to have disappeared entirely."

I considered this for a long moment. "Akzun, there's a word that doctors use on Earth when dealing with certain patients: p*sychosomatic*. Are you familiar with it?"

He shook his head.

"It's when someone thinks they have a medical condition," I went on, "but actually, it's all in their head. They believe it so strongly that their body manifests the symptoms to go along with it. When Elrisa betrayed you, you were filled with grief and rage, but you didn't have a chance to deal with that properly – you had an empire to run, a war to win against the Mana. You could have pushed those feelings away, repressed them to the point where they came to the surface in the form of this bloodlust. But now that you have me… now that you know you're with someone who would never, ever do to you what Elrisa did… maybe you're starting to finally deal with your emotions. Maybe that's why the bloodlust has gone away again."

Akzun nodded thoughtfully. "I believe your theory may indeed be correct. Because I *do* believe in you, Carly. I believe in our love, and our future together."

Love. Hadn't that been exactly what I'd been waiting to hear, and feared I never would? I threw my arms around him, hugging him tightly. "So do I."

"Excellent. And now that you've healed and you're full of new spirit and vitality, what would you like to do next, my beloved mate?"

I grinned. "Oh, I can come up with a few ideas."

I undid his tunic, stroking his smooth, pale chest. He sighed contentedly, shrugging off the tunic and shivering with pure joy. "I will spend the rest of my life doing everything in my power to make you happy, Carly Love."

"You'd better, Blood Ruler," I purred.

He pulled my shirt off, tenderly fondling my breasts with his cold hands – my nipples hardened immediately, and he traced circles around the left one with his thumb, kissing the side of my neck. Goosebumps spread across my skin, and for a moment, I thought he might bite me.

No, darling, he thought, nibbling gently at my earlobe. ***There will be plenty of time for that later. For now, your body must have a chance to heal.***

Fair enough, I thought back, reaching down to cup the bulge that was quickly forming in the front of his trousers. ***We'll just have to think up a few other ways to share fluids, then, won't we?***

Akzun slid my pants down my legs and pushed my thighs apart. He placed his hand between them, feeling how wet I was and licking his lips appreciatively. ***As it happens, I might just have a plan for that.***

He lowered himself on the bed until his head was between my legs and began to kiss my pussy hungrily. I inhaled sharply, tousling his hair, relishing the way he took my clit gently between his teeth and flicked his tongue against it. It felt thrilling and oddly dangerous, like playing with a razorblade – but I knew that I could trust him, that he'd never harm me.

As he licked and teased me, he slid two of his fingers inside me, stimulating my perineum with his knuckles and quickly finding my G-spot with his fingertips. My breath was starting to come in thick, jagged gasps. I couldn't believe how good, how *right*, this felt.

"Oh, Akzun," I moaned, "just like that… yes, please..."

He let out a low chuckle and nodded, his breath tickling my labia. His tongue continued its dance against my most sensitive parts, driving me wild with desire. His fingers kept pushing, pushing, until I saw stars.

I couldn't take any more. I needed him. *All* of him. And what's more, I knew he could read those thoughts from me.

But would he act on them?

Or would he keep teasing me until I lost all control and exploded?

Akzun snickered. ***Perhaps I will give you what you wish, if you beg for it.***

"Please," I panted, "*please*, take me, *fuck* me… "

No. Do not beg me with your lips. Beg me with your mind, your heart. Beg me from the deepest parts of your soul.

I'd never been so turned on before in my life. ***Please, Akzun, take me. Take all of me. Claim every part of me for your own. Make me yours. Your mate.***

He looked up at me, smiling, my juices gleaming on his lips, his chin. ***When you ask me that way, how can I possibly refuse?***

He rose and flipped me onto my belly in a single smooth motion, then positioned himself over me, raking his nails up and down my back. I twitched and moaned, pleading without words, savoring the feel of his hands squeezing my shoulders as he entered me from behind.

After the previous times with him, I'd thought there was no way for him to drive himself even deeper into my pussy – but I was wrong. *So* wrong.

He filled me so completely that he seemed to extend all the way into the pit of my stomach and beyond. I cried out his name over and over like a mantra, gripping the sheets and blankets so hard I could hear them tearing between my fingers.

I *was* stronger now.

Which meant he didn't have to hold back anymore.

His cock slammed inside me like a battering ram, and I felt his breath against the nape of my neck, coming in hot blasts like a furnace. He was giving me everything he had, and I loved it. His pelvis slapped against my buttocks so fast and loud – thrusting, pounding, until my juices frothed thickly against the base of his shaft like sea foam.

You are mine, Carly. And I am yours. Forever.

I felt a radiant heat spread through my body like a star going nova, so intense and powerful that it felt like I would fly apart in a cloud of glittering debris. It was the most forceful orgasm I'd ever experienced, and I felt his a split-second later, gushing through me relentlessly as he called out my name.

Then we were lying in each other's arms, holding on tight enough to make our arms ache.

Chapter Twenty-Four

Akzun

After we'd basked in the glow for a while, I said, "I don't mean to ruin the mood…"

"Then don't," Carly said with a smirk, kissing the tip of my nose.

I smiled. "I'm afraid I must, if only to ask for a description of the person who attacked you earlier."

She sat up, confused. "You mean… you didn't already know? When you didn't ask before, I assumed it was because you caught up with her."

"To be fair, there were more pressing matters for us to discuss," I replied. Then her words caught up to me. "*Her?* You were assaulted by a woman?"

She sighed. "Not just any woman, I'm afraid. You're not going to want to hear this, but – it was Torqa."

"*What?*" I jumped out of bed, enraged. "*Torqa* pushed you down the stairs?"

"Yeah, after trying to filet me with some kind of silver knife."

"Why would she *do* something like that?" I started pacing the room furiously. "She's served Valkred loyally for decades! Why would she betray me now?"

"Because she doesn't think *you're* serving Valkred. She told me everything – how she thought I was making you too weak to lead, how she felt she would be a better mate for you. She's been behind everything, Akzun. All of it. The attack on the Mana ship, the statue that almost fell on me, the thing with the gem mines… I didn't put it together earlier, but I didn't have to. She spelled it all out for me while she was trying to kill me. I would have said something sooner, but I thought she'd already been apprehended."

"By the Succubi, it's all starting to make a terrible kind of sense," I growled. "She had the access, the influence, to make all of that happen. The prisoner she was interrogating killed himself because he knew he couldn't inform us of her involvement… *she* was probably the reason his restraints were loose enough for him to seize the blaster. And the comm system on the Wrath! She'd have known exactly how to disable it remotely, so that we couldn't learn of the threat to the gem mine until we arrived here at the palace. That way, she knew she'd be able to get you alone while Zark and I took care of the saboteurs."

Carly stood up and went to me, putting a hand on my shoulder. "I'm so sorry, Akzun. I know how deeply you're affected by betrayal from the people you trust. You must be hurting a lot right now."

While Carly wasn't incorrect, it went far beyond hurt. Torqa almost took from everything I hold dear. There are no words that can do my rage justice. "Hurting? No. When I catch up with Torqa, it is *she* who will be hurting, and most severely. I will make her pay for what she's done. To repay her for her treatment of you, I will visit tortures upon her far beyond even *her* wildest and most sadistic imaginings."

Carly sighed. "I know, I know. You've got to go after her now, huh? And just when we were starting to have fun."

I thought for a long moment, and then took her by the hand. "Come with me."

I brought Carly to the screen room, and keyed in a set of commands. A holographic image of Zark's head appeared before us almost immediately.

"Brother," Zark greeted us warmly. "And Carly! I'm delighted to see that you've healed from your recent ordeal. Clearly, Khim's talents cannot be overstated."

"I'm afraid I have some rather disturbing news, Zark," I said, wasting no time. "Torqa was the one who attacked Carly."

He let out a low whistle. "By the stars. I knew she was jealous, but I had no idea she'd attempt something so brazen."

"It goes far beyond mere jealousy, brother. She has turned against us. It was *she* who attempted to derail the treaty with the Mana."

Zark's eyes widened, but he nodded slowly. "Of course. How could we have been so blind? Who else could have orchestrated all of these events? She was the most vocal opposition to the ceasefire… she thought it showed weakness, that it would invite other races to attempt war against us. She had motive, means, opportunity. In her own sick way, she probably thought she was proving her loyalty to you and the empire by trying to eliminate Carly and push a decisive victory against the Mana. She always was a diabolical sort. In a peculiar way, one almost has to admire her for almost getting away with it all."

"I certainly hope your admiration won't prevent you from doing what you must in order to subdue her," I said dryly. "Because as of now, apprehending Torqa and bringing her to justice is our foremost priority."

"Naturally. And I assume you're entrusting me with this task?"

I smirked. "Who else?"

"Very well, brother. I won't let you down. Do you happen to have any ideas with regard to where I should look for her? By now, she'll have heard her attempt on Carly's life failed, and she'll have fled the planet – likely the star system, too, for that matter. With her cunning and resources, she could be anywhere."

"She could," I agreed, "but I believe I can suggest a good place to begin your search. Torqa is now a commander without an army. She'll need to find new allies, new cannon fodder for her private war against the Mana – and against us. Mercenaries, no doubt. Raiders. Hired scum. And where might she easily find and recruit such individuals?"

"Cexiea," Zark said without hesitation.

"There, you see? Never mind what our mother used to say – you *are* smarter than you look."

"You're too kind, Blood Ruler," Zark said with a grimace. "I'll begin my hunt for her at once." The hologram shimmered, then blinked out of existence.

"Are you sure you shouldn't go with him?" Carly asked. "I know how important this is to you."

I took her in my arms, kissing her. ***No, my love. I'm right where I'm supposed to be.***

Chapter Twenty-Five

Zark

As soon as I stepped into The Vein, the ugly voice of Nos assaulted my ears, rising above the music and chatter: "Welcome, gentle-beings, yes, yes! Welcome one and all! You seek pretty things for sex, yes? You seek sweet blood to feed upon – mmm, yum yum, tastes good! Makes you big and strong, yes? You have money to pay, much rula for Nos? Then come, make an offer, make a bid, make yourselves happy! Go home with a new plaything, yes? Lonely no more! For tonight is *auction night!*"

Well, damn. I sure picked the wrong night to come looking for Torqa. It'll be difficult to find her in all the crowd and commotion of the auction – and hard to focus, too, with all these pretty blood slaves on display. Plus, the sound of Nos hawking his wares is enough to make me want to puke up every drop of blood I ever drank.

Then again, perhaps this was the best night to search for her. After all, every lowlife in the surrounding twelve star systems tended to show up here on auction night. Some actually came to purchase slaves, but most used the auction to conduct other business unnoticed. Krote pirates, Mana smugglers, ex-pat Valkred bounty hunters and Drekkir hired guns… they all buzzed around eagerly like flies on shit, looking for their next chance to make a quick rula or find their next fix of adrenaline (not to mention any of a dozen other addictive substances).

If Torqa wanted to collect a squad of unsavory characters, this would be the best place for her to do it. And the auction would provide the best cover for her, since she was now one of the most wanted outlaws in the galaxy.

I tried to find her scent, but it was impossible. Too much smoke and sweat, too much bad food and bad breath all around. My eyes cut through the shadows in the corners of the room, searching, but I couldn't find her.

If I started asking around, the clientele here weren't likely to give me straight answers – one or more of them would probably tip her off that someone was looking for her. I was disguised so she wouldn't see me coming, but now what? Plant myself at a table, start knocking back the booze, and wait for her to appear?

I wanted to bring her back so Akzun could punish her, but I was no man hunter. The truth was, I didn't know where to begin.

"Yes, yes, take your seats, esteemed guests, take your places!" Nos announced, gnashing his teeth excitedly. "Time for auction, yes! Big buying! Big spending! Offer up the right price, and all that you desire can be yours for the asking!"

Suddenly, a single scent cut through all the others in the room, digging itself firmly into my brain like a Hykkyan brain parasite.

Human. Female. Intoxicating.

Irresistible.

I shook my head. What was wrong with me? First Akzun loses all control of himself over some Earthling female, and now this? Was there some hereditary disease that was only just manifesting in us both, making us swoon over Earth girls beyond all reason? I had a job to do, damn it. I couldn't let myself be led astray, no matter how tempting she might be, no matter how…

Beautiful.

I saw her at last, and she was *beautiful*.

Long brown hair. Magnificent blue eyes. A tall, powerful, athletic frame. She was standing on the stage behind Nos, waiting for the patrons to bid on her, to claim her.

I couldn't let that happen. I didn't know why, but I couldn't bear the idea of anyone else having her.

She was mine.

I stood up and strode over to the stage, ignoring Nos' outraged cries, and threw the woman over my shoulder. But if I thought she'd go willingly, I was sorely mistaken.

"What the hell is wrong with you?" she demanded immediately, pounding my back with her fists. "Put me down, asshole!"

"Take your hands off her!" Nos chimed in, trying to block my path as I headed for the door. "You bid on her, you win, *then* you have her! Until then, she is *merchandise!* Not to be touched, no, not to be handled before purchase!"

The woman was still pummeling my shoulders, but I could barely feel it past the tingling thrill that was seeping through my veins.

"A quarter of a million rula," I snarled, pushing past Nos. "At least ten times more than you'd get for her at auction. Be sure to send the bill to Akzun, care of the Valkred Empire."

Printed in Dunstable, United Kingdom